Beyond the Tinsel

Beyond the Tinsel

Short Stories for Christmas Eve

DAN SCHOMER

Foreword by Donald K. McKim

RESOURCE *Publications* · Eugene, Oregon

BEYOND THE TINSEL
Short Stories for Christmas Eve

Resource Publications
An Imprint of Wipf and Stock Publishers
199 W. 8th Ave., Suite 3
Eugene, OR 97401

www.wipfandstock.com

PAPERBACK ISBN: 978-1-6667-0574-4
HARDCOVER ISBN: 978-1-6667-0575-1
EBOOK ISBN: 978-1-6667-0576-8

04/28/21

To Joan,

my wife,

my love, my life,

a loving mother,

an adoring Nana,

a dedicated special education teacher, now retired,

my best friend.

Contents

Foreword

Stories intrigue us. From earliest days, children often say to their parents, "Tell me a story." Even as we grow older, stories continue to have their appeal. They draw us in. They create a world in our minds and hearts as we follow the paths the stories lay before us. We are drawn to their characters, the actions and decisions made throughout the narrative. We envision circumstances of the story with pleasure, anticipating what might happen next, and after the story is completed we reflect on it with satisfaction and continuing delight. Stories fascinate us!

Things happen in stories. There is the action of the story and its characters, but there are also things that happen to us, the listeners or readers. Stories have power. They can form and shape our understandings. Stories can move us to action. Stories can reveal new insights, insights that might not come to us in any other ways. Stories can penetrate our thoughts and reveal things to us about ourselves, our cultures, and our world that we would not recognize otherwise. Stories act on us in moving and memorable ways.

When we recognize the power of stories we will realize how important the stories Dan Schomer tells in this book turn out to be. Dan, my friend since our days together in college, is an accomplished preacher and church leader. His Christmas Eve sermons, collected here, are interesting and fascinating. They are a beautiful gift. Dan masterfully engages us in each story, taking us back to the days and events surrounding the birth of Jesus of Nazareth to Mary and Joseph. The familiar biblical story of Jesus' nativity comes alive here in wider and biblically responsible ways. We are introduced in short stories to how characters and events in the Christmas story can take on further life as we hear of reactions and responses to the events surrounding Jesus' birth. We are told stories of our Christmas experience today which reflect back and witness to the first Christmas and what it means. Dan uses what can be called "sanctified imagination" to open new worlds of insight and understandings for us through these thoroughly appealing narratives of memorable characters!

But these stories do more than just give us something interesting to hear. They can deepen our Christian faith and perception of the glorious message of the coming of Jesus Christ into the world to embody and show God's love. As Dan tells us: "The stories that follow are inspired by a wonderful and powerful mystery described in John 1:14: "And the Word became flesh and lived among us, and we have seen his glory, the glory as of a father's only son, full of grace and truth." True to this inspiration throughout, each story illuminates aspects of the biblical story and the theological truths to which they point, in biblical times and today. This gives the stories power to affect us in significant ways. The stories can deepen our understandings of this mystery of God come among us humans in the person of God's Son, Jesus Christ. In realizing this glorious message of the Christian gospel, our lives can be shaped. We can be moved to new thoughts and actions that can provide meaning and fresh directions in life. These stories have power to shape our consciousness and reveal insights that move us into receiving the grace and truth God wishes to give us.

These endearing stories can not only warm our hearts, they can also change our lives. The stories have power because they are focused on the powerful message of the Christmas story: God's Word, Jesus Christ, became a human being, and lived among us! This is "good news"—gospel. Stories that witness to this gospel are stories that are powerful and life-changing!

Dan Schomer's stories may not seem to be dramatic and may not appear to affect us spectacularly. But "the way of Jesus" is usually more subtle, being at work in "small ways," in the midst of our everyday lives. Like the parables Jesus told, so the gospel message of Jesus himself takes shape and works its power in the world around us where the power of love is supreme. It can be expressed in ways that bring comfort and peace, even in a "cup of cold water" (Matt 10:42).

So let these beautiful stories help you go beyond the tinsel at Christmas. Enjoy their beauty, receive the power and blessings they convey. Let these wonderful stories bring you "good news of great joy" (Luke 2:10), the news of the "Savior, who is the Messiah, the Lord!" (Luke 2:11).

Donald K. McKim
Germantown, Tennessee

Preface

The stories that follow are inspired by a wonderful and powerful mystery described in John 1:14: "And the Word became flesh and lived among us, and we have seen his glory, the glory as of a father's only son, full of grace and truth." As I wrote these short stories, what emerged over the years was an enduring confidence in a God who is with us, especially the humble among us, and whose love is manifest both in us and through us. Jesus tells us the will of God is summed up in the mandate to love God above all else and love neighbor as self. In these stories, I seek to affirm that our humble, imperfect, sometime feeble attempts to love others changes lives and establishes the kingdom or realm of God. Beyond the tinsel, we discover the incarnation of the Lord to be the gift that keeps on giving.

I am grateful to the late C. Kenneth Hall, longtime pastor of the Hill Presbyterian Church in Butler, Pennsylvania, and Moderator of the 200th General Assembly of the Presbyterian Church (U.S.A.), who taught me the power of a story on Christmas Eve. I am thankful for the insights gained from the late Dr. Kenneth E. Bailey, under whom I studied in pursuit of a Doctor of Ministry at McCormick Theological Seminary. I am also grateful to Dr. Donald K. McKim, who has guided me through the process of having a book published. Thank you to the New Sewickley United Presbyterian Church in New Brighton, Pennsylvania, and the First Presbyterian Church in Columbiana, Ohio, for their encouragement of my storytelling. Most of all, I thank my wife Joan, my children

Eileen, Erin, and Matthew, my son-in-law Daniel, my daughter-in-law Tara, and my grandchildren Benjamin, Ora, and Lucy, for their love and inspiration.

Introduction

There is something about Christmas that invites a story. The theological heart of the Christian faith is found in the narratives we revisit each year in the Lent—Holy Week—Easter texts in the four Gospels. In these four related yet distinct narratives, we are provided with great details about the week that begins with Palm Sunday and begins again with the resurrection of Jesus.

Yet, when we turn to the four Gospels in search of narratives about the birth of Jesus, there are far fewer details. In the first two chapters of the Gospel of Matthew we find a brief birth narrative followed by a more detailed story of the visit of the magi and the slaughter of the innocents in Bethlehem. In the first two chapters of the Gospel of Luke we find the narratives that form the heart of the Christmas story—the annunciation to Mary, the decree of Caesar Augustus, the journey to Bethlehem, the birth of the Christ child, the angelic invitation to the shepherds, and their arrival at the manger. The opening verses of John's Gospel provide a magnificent reflection on the significance of the incarnation, but do not give a single detail of Jesus' birth. The Gospel of Mark says nothing at all about the birth of Jesus. At best, the Gospels provide hints and thumbnail sketches, leaving a great deal to the imagination.

When I was ordained as a minister in 1975 in what is now the Presbyterian Church (U.S.A.), I especially looked forward to my first Christmas Eve service. For me, Christmas Eve candlelight services had been a highlight of the Christmas season for as long as I could remember, and now I had the opportunity to make it so for the congregations I served. But how? I decided to draw from those Christmas Eve worship experiences I had found most meaningful. Among those experiences was the practice of my home pastor in Butler, Pennsylvania, Ken Hall, who would select and tell a Christmas story in place of a sermon. Ken was a superb preacher and carefully explored the biblical texts related to Advent and Christmastide each Sunday; but on Christmas Eve, he would memorize a story and share it with those gathered for worship.

I also chose to replace the sermon with a story on Christmas Eve. I spent many hours researching and selecting a story that would spark the imagination while also communicating the inspiration found in the biblical narratives. After the first few years, I decided I would try my hand at writing the Christmas stories with the same goals of including imagination and inspiration. Over the years, the stories were received with enthusiasm and appreciation by the congregations I served.

As I reviewed these stories written between 1975 and 2003, I discovered details that no longer fit my interpretation of the birth narratives. My introduction to the work of Dr. Kenneth Bailey in the early 1990s dramatically altered the way I interpret the Christmas story. Dr. Bailey, a noted biblical scholar who spent much of his ministry in the Middle East, helps us view the biblical text through first-century Middle Eastern eyes. Two key points from Bailey's work on the birth narratives that have significantly changed my understanding of Luke 2:1–20 are the meaning of the inn and the manger.

In Luke 2:7, we read, "And she gave birth to her firstborn son and wrapped him in bands of cloth and laid him in a *manger* because there was no place for them in the *inn*." In Western culture, the generally accepted interpretation of Luke's Gospel is that Mary and Joseph could not find room at a commercial inn and therefore found it necessary to take refuge in the inn's stable where Jesus was born. In the stories I wrote set in biblical times, I assumed these details and incorporated them into the narrative. Dr. Bailey's work moved me to rewrite these stories to incorporate the insights I gained from studying his works.

Bailey tells us that our traditional Western version of the birth narrative would have seemed strange to the first-century Middle Eastern reader. Bailey points out that in Luke 2:7 the Greek word *kataluma* is incorrectly translated as "inn" in most English translations. Bailey concludes that a better translation for *kataluma* is "guest room." It appears that this latter translation is the one intended by Luke. When Luke wants to speak of a commercial inn providing shelter for strangers as in the parable of the good Samaritan (10:34), he uses the Greek word *pandokheion*. In Luke 22:11, when Jesus gives instructions concerning where he and his disciples will celebrate the Passover, Luke again uses *kataluma* to describe an upper "guest room" that was attached to a house.

Applying Luke's choice of words to what we learn from Dr. Bailey about first-century Middle Eastern homes provides a setting for the birth of Jesus that is quite different from the traditional one of a stable behind the inn. According to Bailey and other authoritative sources he cites, Palestinian homes in the first century were normally one-room, split-level structures. About 80 percent of the home was the living area where the family lived, ate, and slept. Normally the living area was elevated several feet above ground level. The remaining area at ground level was blocked off and used to house the livestock overnight. Many homes also had a *kataluma*, a private guest room attached to the home, sometimes on the flat roof.

But even if we do accept "there was no room for them in the guest room" as the correct translation, how does Bailey explain the manger? Luke specifically says that Jesus' first crib was a manger—a food trough for livestock. Wouldn't a manger be found in a stable? Bailey responds that at the edge of the terraced living area of the home, mangers were built into the floor which were several feet above the area where the animals were housed. "If the family cow is hungry through the night, she can stand up and eat from mangers cut out of the floor of the living room. Mangers for sheep can be of wood and placed on the floor of the lower level."[1] Each morning the livestock were led outside and the area where they

1. Bailey, *Jesus through Middle Eastern Eyes*, 30.

were housed was thoroughly cleaned. At night they were brought back inside. Bailey suggests that such a manger in the living area of a first-century Middle Eastern home would have provided a convenient place to safely hold a newborn.

Dr. Bailey's knowledge of ancient Middle Eastern culture also provides strong support for his interpretation of *kataluma* and the location of the manger. Hospitality was considered a sacred duty. Bethlehem was Joseph's ancestral home. One who was of the house and lineage of David would have no doubt found welcome in any home in the city of David. If the guest room was already occupied, the family living there would have extended hospitality to the holy family by sharing the main living space of the home with them. Thus, instead of huddling in the isolation of a stable with their newborn, Joseph, Mary, and the Christ child are pictured as enjoying the warm hospitality of a Palestinian home and family.

Bailey summarizes:

> A part of what Luke tells about the birth of Jesus is that the holy family traveled to Bethlehem, where they were received into a private home. The child was born, wrapped and (literally) "put to bed" (*anaklinō*) in the living room in the manger that was either built into the floor or made of wood and moved into the family living space. Why weren't they invited into the family guest room, the reader might naturally ask? The answer is that the guest room was already occupied by other guests. The host family graciously accepted Mary and Joseph into the family room of their house.[2]

Dr. Bailey's greatest contribution to our understanding of the birth narrative is the sharp contrast he provides to the traditional Western understanding of Jesus' birth. Rather than rejection of the Christ child for whom there is no room, Bailey envisions a warm welcoming of the holy family by the humble, who were likewise poor and oppressed. Note that the humble, poor, and oppressed peasantry were those who first followed Jesus and comprised the early church.

2. Bailey, *Jesus Through Middle Eastern Eyes*, 34.

As you read these stories, I invite you to imagine the setting of a warm but humble peasant home rather than an isolated stable for the birth of Jesus. Each story emphasizes that, as God chooses a humble setting for the holy birth, so too the humble and seemingly insignificant are those through whom God establishes the kingdom of God. A recurring theme throughout these stories is the contrast between an empire, whose values are characterized by power and domination, and the kingdom of God, whose values function like leaven and a mustard seed. Beyond the tinsel, the incarnation of the Lord is about the self-giving love of God that is manifest in us through self-giving love for others.

The stories are organized into three sections. In the *Imagine* section, you are invited to listen to conversations between angels, look at the world through the eyes of a donkey, consider what thoughts an evergreen tree might have as Christmas draws near, and listen to a story within a story as a grandfather seeks to entertain his little granddaughter while waiting for the candlelight service to begin. The *At the Manger* section contains stories that describe firsthand experiences of the birth of Jesus by fictional characters who fit the time and culture of the birth narratives. In the section *A Homespun Christmas*, you will find Christmas stories that coincide with our times and culture. My hope is that these stories will provide you with some holiday enjoyment while also giving you something to ponder as you explore the deeper meaning of the birth of Jesus.

This book can be used in a variety of way.

Personal devotions. Daily personal devotions provide a spiritual discipline for many Christians. The reading of a story along with a Scripture reading can serve as an enriching daily spiritual exercise. The *Revised Common Lectionary* provides daily Scripture readings that follow the church calendar.

Group devotions. Many groups, organizations, boards, committees, and fellowship gatherings begin with a group devotional. The stories within this book provide an easy resource for opening devotions.

Worship. Each story was originally written as the evening message for a Christmas Eve worship service. Pastors and worship leaders may desire to share one of these stories in lieu of preparing and preaching a sermon.

Christian education. These stories can be used for study and reflection by both children and adults in a Christian education setting.

Questions for Reflection and Discussion are provided at the end of each chapter. The questions can be used for personal reflection, journaling, and group discussion.

Imagine

1. The Final Invitation

Her name was Gloria. As angels go, she was rather run-of-the-mill. She had special gifts as did all the angels, but she wasn't the brightest star in the sky. No one tried harder; but when you are an angel, some important matters are entrusted to you. Gloria's performance was sometimes little more than passing.

But Gloria was determined she would get it right this time. She didn't know what assignment she would be given, but she would strive to carry it out superbly. Gabriel and Michael would have nothing on her this time. It was the event that had been anticipated since the universe had been created by the Lord God. It was the time that the prophets of Israel had proclaimed for generations. God would send the Son into the world as a human child. Just thinking about it made Gloria so excited that she found herself flying around uncontrollably.

It was while Gloria was pondering her role in the holy birth that Michael, the archangel, tapped her on the wing. She startled for a moment and then turned to see a stern look on Michael's face.

"Gloria, we're waiting."

Gloria sprang to her feet and obediently followed Michael to the great assembly hall. How could she have lost track of time? How could she have allowed daydreaming to interfere with this most important of heavenly assemblies? As she entered the great hall, all eyes were on her. She bowed her head and mumbled, "Sorry."

The radiance of the face of the Almighty quickly calmed her. The voice of the Lord God began to speak, sounding like the rolling of thunder and the gentle singing of a lullaby all at the same time.

"My messengers, the time has come for the holy birth. Each of you have a role to play. As I call your name, I will give you your assignment. Go quickly, for the time is near."

The Lord God began calling names and giving specific assignments. Would Gloria be called to join the angelic choir, singing glory to God and goodwill to humankind? Name after name was called, but Gloria's was not among them. Would Gloria be privileged to proclaim the holy birth to prominent people on earth? Again, Gloria's name was not spoken.

Finally, Gloria stood alone in the great assembly hall in the presence of the Lord God. Bowing low, she said, "Please, Almighty Sovereign, Creator of heaven and earth, is there not something I can do?"

The voice of God responded, "Gloria, my child, you have not been gifted with song." Gloria knew this, for she could not carry a tune if all eternity depended upon it. "And you do not have the voice for proclamation." Gloria also knew this truth, for her voice was high and a bit squeaky. "But Gloria, my child, when I created you, I gave you a heart that is warmer and gentler than any other angel. Therefore, I do not send you to sing to my Son's glory, nor do I assign you to proclaim with words the meaning of his birth. Instead, I entrust you with these invitations to come and celebrate the holy birth. They are for a select few. These invitations will not speak to their minds, but will touch their hearts, beckoning them to come and behold my newborn Son."

Gloria reached out her hands and received the invitations with expressions of gratitude for the Lord God's trust in her. As she departed the great assembly hall, she began looking through the invitations. She was surprised at how few there were. She expected to find the names of the great leaders of the nations. Where was the invitation for Caesar? She tried to imagine the face of the Emperor of Rome at the news that God's Son had come to reign on earth.

What about the invitation for King Herod, that old scoundrel, and for the high priest who presided at the temple in Jerusalem? Would they not be brought to their knees before God's Son?

But the invitations Gloria expected were not there. The first invitation was addressed to Mary of Nazareth. She arrived at the humble home just as Gabriel was leaving. As Gloria entered, she found a young girl quite distraught. As she reached toward Mary with the invitation, it became like incense in her hand and a peaceful expression came across Mary's face.

"Let it be," she whispered.

Next, she took the invitation addressed to Joseph of Nazareth. She could not help but notice the signs of a hard-working man—carpentry tools and calloused hands. As she drew nearer, Gloria found Joseph in fitful sleep. She placed the invitation in his hand. He opened his eyes and she heard him utter, "I now believe and know what I must do."

Her next destination was a hillside in Bethlehem. The angelic choir was just finishing their "Glory to God in the Highest." The faces of the shepherds revealed pure terror and Gloria feared they would run away before she had the opportunity to deliver her invitation. Much to her delight, as she held out the invitation, the shepherds calmed down. They looked at one another and proclaimed, "Let us go and see the child."

Her next invitation was carried to the east to a group of men who were dressed in strange clothing and were pointing to a particular star in the sky. As she reached out with the invitation, they declared, "We must go and pay homage to the newborn king."

As Gloria looked at the final invitation, she was bewildered. The name of the recipient was blank. Nothing had been written upon it. "How odd," she thought. She had never known the Lord God to be forgetful, but what was she supposed to do with the final invitation?

As she gazed at the anonymous invitation, it suddenly occurred to her—this was an opportunity to redeem herself for all the mistakes she had made in the past. Now she understood why there was no invitation to the Emperor of Rome. This must be it.

She flew with haste and entered the palace of the emperor. With pride she held out the invitation to Caesar, but the invitation remained in her hand. Clearly this invitation was not for him. Next, she made her way to the palace of King Herod. Surely the Lord God wanted the king of the Jews informed of the birth of the true King of Israel. But once again, the invitation remained in her outstretched hand and once again there was no response. Perplexed, Gloria decided to try one more time. She went to the temple in Jerusalem and approached the high priest who was burning incense at the altar. She reached out her hand, but the invitation remained there.

A frown came over Gloria's countenance. She bowed her head like a child who had received a poor grade on a school paper and returned to the heavenly realm, the anonymous invitation still in her hand. As she neared the throne room, a strong wind came along and lifted the invitation from her hand. Frantically, she looked for it, but it had drifted from her sight. Gloria was suddenly overcome with a sense of panic. What would she do? Not only had she failed to deliver the final invitation, but she had lost it.

She was just about to turn and go the other way when that familiar powerful and sweet voice spoke her name. "Gloria."

Slowly she turned and answered, "Yes, my Lord."

"Come and tell me, have you completed your deliveries?"

Gloria slowly approached the throne of grace. Her head was bowed and she could not look into the face of the Almighty.

"My Creator and Lord," she began, "I delivered the invitations to Nazareth, to a woman named Mary and a man named Joseph. I took the invitation to the shepherds in Bethlehem and the wise men in the east. It was clear to me that their hearts received the invitation and there is a place in their hearts for your Son to be born. But the final invitation . . ." She stopped for a moment to collect her thoughts. "I tried to deliver the final invitation and," she gulped, "I failed."

"What do you mean, my child?" asked the voice that was more gentle than powerful this time.

"The invitation was not addressed. I tried to determine to whom it might belong. First, I took it to Caesar, then to Herod, and then the high priest, but their hearts were not touched. Their hearts refused your invitation. I was on my way to return the final invitation to you when a strong wind snatched it from my hand. I tried to find it, but I couldn't."

Suddenly, Gloria was startled by the sound of laughter, a delightful laughter that Gloria had never heard come from the throne of grace. "My child, you did deliver the final invitation. It was not for the emperor or Herod or the high priest."

"But Lord, I didn't deliver the final invitation. I lost it!" exclaimed Gloria. "A strong wind blew it from my hand."

"That was no wind," responded the Lord God, "it was my breath. The final invitation was for the whole world, to hearts everywhere that are open to the love and grace of my Son. My child, you did complete your assignment and have fulfilled your commission. In fact, dear Gloria, you are the only one of my angels in whom I would entrust this most important responsibility. From this time forth, on the night when we celebrate my Son's humble birth, I will give you an invitation. You will hold up the invitation and I will breathe upon it. As my breath carries it away, hearts everywhere that are open to me will be touched again with the desire to come and worship the Christ."

So, in this holy season, when you find your heart touched and transformed by the scene of the holy family in humble surroundings and a child who reveals the face of God, it might just be a divine invitation to your heart to come and worship the newborn king delivered by a humble messenger of God.

Questions for Reflection and Discussion:

1. Gloria thinks the voice of God sounds like the rolling of thunder and the gentle singing of a lullaby. What does the voice of God sound like to you? How do you hear the voice of God?

2. How do we listen both with our minds and our hearts? What does each provide to guide us in our important decisions?

3. Remember a time when God surprised you by working through you. What happened? What surprised you? How does this experience motivate you in your spiritual journey?

2. A Christmas Lullaby

She sat at her desk with pen in hand, putting the finishing touches on the anthem she had spent so long completing. This would be her greatest work. She was sure of it. Note by note, word by word, stanza by stanza, she reviewed the anthem. "Everything must be right," she thought. "Everything must be perfect."

Her name was Chara. She was the angelic choirmaster. Her name literally meant "joy," and it is an appropriate name for her. Over the centuries, the songs her choir of angels sang to women and men of faith brought joy to their hearts, even in the midst of hopeless and desperate situations.

Chara was interrupted by a knock at her chamber door, and she responded with a half-annoyed, "Come in."

The door slowly swung open and there stood Gabriel. Chara and Gabriel had worked closely together during recent months. When Gabriel was given an especially important assignment from the Lord God, he often came to Chara to ask her to write a special song of praise or rejoicing. Songs had been written for Elizabeth and Zechariah. She was especially proud of the song she had composed for Mary. Now she was preparing the greatest of all heavenly anthems—the one announcing the birth of the Messiah.

"Gabriel, my friend, what can I do for you?" she inquired.

"Dear Chara, I am checking to see how the anthem is coming," answered Gabriel with some apprehension. He could not remember when so much of Chara's time had been consumed by one assignment.

Chara smiled an exhausted smile and held up a golden scroll. "It is finished," she beamed. "The choir begins practice tomorrow." Gabriel smiled broadly. "Wonderful," he said, half-excited, half-relieved. "Wonderful. Well, I'll let you get on with your work." With that, Gabriel left Chara's chamber.

Chara sat embracing the scroll upon which she had written her angelic anthem. She tried to imagine what it would be like to lead the choir in her finest composition. "Glory to God in the highest heaven, and on earth peace."[1] Chara wondered where the choir would be assigned to sing these words of rejoicing. She imagined the choir of angels hovering over the temple in Jerusalem. Imagine the look of amazement on the faces of the priests when the birth of the Messiah was announced. The splendid temple would be overshadowed by the splendor of her angelic choir. Or perhaps the Lord God had chosen to have her choir overwhelm the emperor and his court in Rome. The one who had the audacity to claim to be a god himself would be quaking in his toga at the news that God's Son had been born. And what a splendid sight it would be to gaze upon the newborn Messiah! Surely the splendor of his royal nursery would be overwhelming, revealing his glorious heritage. Kings and queens of all nations would fall to their knees before him in fear and trembling. "Glory to God in the highest heaven, and on earth peace." Yes, it would be a glorious moment indeed.

Chara's thoughts were interrupted when her chamber door slowly began to open, and she again heard Gabriel's voice calling her name half-apologetically. Chara invited Gabriel in and inquired, "What brings you back so soon?"

"Dear, dear Chara," he began. She knew she was in trouble right away. A double "dear" before her name always meant Gabriel was about to ask a big favor. "When I came to your chamber before, it was to tell you of another assignment. I was so excited about the completion of the anthem that I forgot to ask . . . ."

"Another assignment?" interrupted Chara. "I have worked day and night for weeks on this anthem; I begin rehearsals

1. Luke 2:14a.

tomorrow; the time draws near for its performance; and you come with another assignment? Gabriel, you ask too much."

"I do not ask," responded Gabriel. His words almost sounded like a prayer. "The request comes directly from the throne of glory."

Chara looked startled and said nothing for a few moments. Then in a soft, controlled voice she asked, "What does the Lord God want me to do?"

"A lullaby," answered Gabriel. "The Lord God wants you to write a lullaby to calm and comfort the newborn king."

"A lullaby," Chara repeated. She thought for a moment and her wrinkled brow gave way to a half-smile. "A lullaby," she repeated. This time there was a touch of delight in her voice. "Please tell the Lord God it would be my greatest privilege to write a lullaby for his Son."

Gabriel, startled by the ease with which he had delivered the message and received a response, left the chamber without a word.

"A lullaby," Chara repeated to herself. *A lullaby for Mary to sing to her newborn son as she rocks him to sleep for the first time,* she supposed. "What a privilege," she said out loud and was startled by the sound of her own voice. She reached for another scroll and slowly began to write a lullaby fit for the Son of God.

Weeks passed. The choir of angels was weary due to the marathon practices Chara had demanded of them. The lullaby was ready to bring comfort and reassurance to the newborn king. All that remained were the final instructions from the throne of glory and the great event would unfold.

When the moment did arrive, all participants were assembled together. There was Chara, standing straight and tall in front of her choir, beaming with anticipation as Gabriel entered the assembly hall. Gabriel raised his arm, clearly displaying a golden scroll in hand. All grew silent when they saw the royal seal, meaning these instructions had come from the very hand of God. Ceremoniously, Gabriel broke the seal and began to read. He said nothing. His eyes were fixed on the scroll for what seemed an eternity.

Finally, Chara could contain herself no longer. "What is our destination, Gabriel? Please tell us. Is it Jerusalem?"

"No," Gabriel muttered hesitantly.

Chara's eyes lit up. "Then it's," she swallowed hard and continued, "it's Rome, isn't it? We're going to the very center of the earthly empire to make our birth announcement."

"No!" responded Gabriel a bit more emphatically this time. "We are going," Gabriel paused for a brief moment, "to Bethlehem."

"Bethlehem?" blurted out Chara. "But Gabriel, who is in Bethlehem but shepherd and sheep?"

Chara hoped her worst fears were unfounded, but the look in Gabriel's eyes heightened her concern.

This time, reading the royal decree with clarity and confidence, he declared to Chara and the heavenly host, "You shall go to Bethlehem to announce the birth of the Messiah to shepherds watching their flocks. Thus, declares the Sovereign Lord."

Chara tried to hide her disappointment, but her scowl gave away her emotions. Gabriel looked her straight in the eye and walked in her direction. He stopped a few feet in front of her. "I know you are disappointed," he whispered. "I am as surprised as you," he continued, "but maybe this will make up for it." Gabriel reached into the pocket of his robe and pulled out a small scroll containing the royal seal.

The lullaby. In all the excitement, surprise and disappointment, Chara had forgotten about the lullaby. But just as she was about to open it, an archangel arrived from the very presence of God to declare, "It is time. Fulfill your assignment to the glory of Almighty God who sits upon the throne."

Chara hurriedly tucked the little scroll in her robe. She turned to give orders to her angelic choir who nervously assembled and prepared for their all-important performance. The plan was this— Gabriel would precede them, announcing the good news of great joy for all the people. After the formal birth announcement, Chara would move the choir into position to sing their heavenly anthem to the glory of God and in celebration of the holy birth.

Chara was disappointed to discover their audience consisted of just eleven shepherds. It was growing late by earthly calculations, and half of them were asleep. The others were wandering, not too far from the campfire, making sure the sheep were safe from predators or thieves. At the sight of Gabriel and the glory of the Lord that surrounded him, the shepherds nearly jumped out of their skins. Those who were asleep awoke with a start. One tried to get to his feet and, in the process, caught them in his own robe. He hit the ground as though he had been tackled. Another was so startled that he ran off into the night. Those who jumped to their feet now fell on their faces in terror.

"Do not be afraid," Gabriel declared, but it was too late. These shepherds were visibly shaking. "I am bringing you good news of great joy for all the people."[2] Gabriel continued his birth announcement. He told them that the Savior, the long-awaited Messiah, had been born that very day in their town of Bethlehem. They would know they had found him when they discovered a newborn wrapped in swaddling clothes and lying in a manger.

"Swaddling clothes?" Chara whispered to herself. "A manger?" This couldn't be right. The Messiah, the Savior, the Son of God should be born in a palace and laid in a crib of finest gold.

While Chara struggled with this strange good news, she almost missed her cue. Just in the nick of time she gained her composure and moved her choir into place. At the very first note of the heavenly anthem, the shepherds, whom Gabriel had managed to half calm down, went into another panic. Those who had made it to their knees again hit the ground, face-down. The anthem continued, but Chara wondered if the tiny audience even heard a note. As the choir sang the final stanza, Chara motioned for all to depart. Suddenly the shepherds were alone in the dark and the silence, their hearts pounding, and their heads filled with strange and wonderful good news.

Chara thanked her choir for their fine performance and the choir members quickly dispersed, as confused as the choirmaster. Chara was about to return to her chamber when she felt the little scroll she had tucked in her robe. "The lullaby," she remembered, "I must go and teach the lullaby to Mary so she may sing it to the newborn Messiah."

2. Luke 2:10b.

Chara made her way back to Bethlehem and found the house where the holy family was staying. There she beheld Mary, Joseph, and the lovely child, and her heart swelled with joy. To her surprise the shepherds were there too. Apparently, despite all the confusion, they had gotten the message and had come to witness this miraculous event.

Chara prepared to approach Mary and whisper the lullaby in her ear, that she might sing it to the holy child, when she was distracted by the entrance of a man and a little girl. The man bowed low in front of Joseph and spoke. "Good sir, we live across the way. My daughter, Rebekah, found out about the birth of your child and desires to see him. Please excuse her silence, but she can neither hear nor speak. She was born that way. May she just take a peek and then we will leave you to rest?"

Mary nodded and Joseph invited her to come and see their new baby. The girl looked up at her father and, with an approving smile, he gently nudged her forward. Slowly, almost reverently, she approached the manger that had become a cradle. She gazed with wonder at the tiny baby lying in a manger. Though she did not utter a sound, the expression on her face said what words could never say. She had not received an angelic birth announcement like the shepherds or heard Chara's anthem sung by the choir of angels. Yet, the wonderment in her eyes and the joy upon her face declared that she somehow realized the specialness of this moment. That's when Chara moved forward, silently, invisibly, to teach her lullaby. But instead of going to Mary, she knelt beside the child. In an angelic voice that could only be heard by the heart of a silent little girl, she began to sing her beloved lullaby. And suddenly, to the total amazement of all, the child began to repeat the song, word by word, note by note, line by line. When the last note had been sung, Chara gave the child an angelic kiss, and quickly departed.

A quiet knock announced that someone was at Chara's door. She sat silently in her chamber and did not acknowledge the visitor. After several more attempts the door opened and there was Gabriel.

"Chara, what's wrong?" pleaded Gabriel. Why didn't you answer the door?"

Chara looked visibly shaken. "I have disobeyed divine orders," she groaned and held out the little golden scroll with the royal seal still visibly in place. "I know I was to teach the lullaby to Mary, but I did not. I taught it to another."

Gabriel took two steps forward and reach out to take the scroll. He broke the seal, opened it, and read it. He looked at Chara, then at the scroll, then at Chara again. "It says nothing here about teaching the lullaby to Mary," Gabriel said, clearly confused.

Chara took the scroll from Gabriel's hand. There was written, "Teach the lullaby prepared for the Messiah to the child Rebekah, whom I have invited." A gentle smile came to Chara's face and she now finally understood. The newborn Messiah had not come into the world to impress high priests or visit emperors. He had come for the sake of the humble and lowly, the frightened and the broken. And, on this holy night, it was clear he had come into the world for a little girl whose childlike wonderment and faith resulted in a surprising Christmas lullaby.

Questions for Reflection and Discussion

1. If Jesus were to be born into today's world, where do you think it would it be? Why?

2. How do the birth narratives in the Gospels of Matthew and Luke inform your understanding of power?

3. When has an encounter with a humble person or humble surroundings been transformational for you?

3. The Surprising Hero of Christmas

On a cold winter night, as frigid rain pelted against the roof of the stable and a chilly wind blew, he came into the world. Benjamin was the first to discover the newborn. He entered with a lantern held high, straining to see the occupants of the stall. He spied the newborn lying in the straw. "Father, Father, come quick," he shouted. "The foal is here."

Caleb entered the stable still chewing the last bite of his dinner. "Where is it, Son?" Benjamin pointed to a stall in the corner and followed his father as he drew closer.

"Oh my," exclaimed Caleb with a start. "Oh my," he repeated.

Before them, lying in the straw, was the ugliest newborn donkey he had ever seen. The poor creature looked like he had collided with a wagon of paint—blotches of grey, white, and brown covering his skinning body. His one ear was decidedly longer than the other, one standing straight up and the other drooped down. His eyes were misaligned giving him the appearance of being cross-eyed.

"Father," Benjamin began, "what shall we name him?"

Caleb just stared at the little creature. "Son, I will not waste a name on an animal that looks like that."

Caleb had been hoping for a fine animal that would bring a hefty price. Caleb raised donkeys for a living and it had been a lean year. Fewer colts had been born that year than he could remember. Caleb's disgust at the appearance of this newest addition to his stable was mixed with concern that he might not be able to sell him at any price.

Weeks passed, then months, and the little donkey with no name grew. Unfortunately, as he grew larger, he also grew uglier. Even the other donkeys seemed to want to keep their distance. All, of course, except his mother. He may have had a face only a mother could love, but she loved him completely. To Little No Name, the rejection of the others and Caleb's harsh words were insignificant as long as his mother was near.

But even this small bit of consolation was taken away. Caleb had needed money and was forced to thin the herd. His mother was the only female to be sold. "After all," Caleb had said, "if she bears offspring like this one, she's no good to me for breeding."

Now the little donkey with no name felt really, truly, totally alone. He stood all day in a dark corner of the stable, his head down, his droopy ear falling over one eye. He had little appetite, as his skinny frame revealed. If an animal can feel despair, the ugly little donkey was consumed by it.

Once, Caleb had been forced to use him to carry some goods from Nazareth to nearby Capernaum. The donkey had half-heartedly done what was expected; but when you have been told repeatedly that you are worthless, your efforts tend to fall short. "I should have drowned you the day you were born, you worthless beast," Caleb shouted as he returned the donkey with no name to the stable. "You have no spirit."

Before long, business picked up for Caleb. Suddenly his donkeys were in great demand. Caesar Augustus, Emperor of Rome, had decreed that everyone within the empire must go to their ancestral home to be enrolled. How ironic that an action by the hated Roman emperor would result in the closest thing to prosperity that Caleb had experienced. The mandated enrollment would require many citizens from Nazareth to travel substantial distances to complete the enrollment, making beasts of burden particularly attractive. Soon, the only donkey left in the stable was the one with no name.

In the early morning hours, Caleb heard someone knocking on his door. "Caleb? Caleb? Are you home?" the voice outside cried. Slowly the door opened, sending a cool breath of morning air into the house.

"Joseph, what brings you to my home so early in the morning?"

"Caleb, I need a donkey," Joseph responded. "Mary and I must go to my ancestral home of Bethlehem for the enrollment. The journey is a long one and Mary is with child. I don't want her walking all that way."

"Joseph, I wish I could help you, but . . ." Caleb stopped short. "I do have one donkey," Caleb paused for a moment, "but he's my favorite. I hate to part with him." Caleb led Joseph into the stable. There in one corner was the dejected beast. "A fine animal," Caleb kept saying.

"What is his name?" asked Joseph.

"His name?" Caleb repeated. After stalling for a moment, he replied, "His name is Gabriel. It means 'hero of God,' you know."

The donkey raised his head in surprise, one ear turned toward Caleb. The donkey looked around the empty stable. Who could Caleb be speaking about?

"Joseph," Caleb continued, "because we've been neighbors for so long and you have such a great need for a donkey, I will sell this fine beast to you for just twenty denarii."

"Caleb, I need this donkey," replied Joseph looking firmly into Caleb's eyes, "but I only have fifteen denarii to spare."

Caleb, who had never hoped to get more than four or five denarii at best for him, looked at the ground, shuffling his feet in the dust as though he were deep in thought. Finally, he raised his head.

"Joseph, you drive a hard bargain and I wouldn't do this for just anyone, but he's yours for fifteen denarii." Caleb was paid and Joseph began leading Gabriel out of the stable. "Oh Joseph," Caleb said as he walked away. "Such a fine bargain can have no guarantees." Gabriel's head dropped as he was led away by Joseph.

When Gabriel arrived at the home of his new master, they were met by a young woman who, it was clear, was going to have a baby. Mary scratched him between the ears as she smiled at the funny-looking donkey with the curious name. It was the first sign of affection shown Gabriel in many months.

When it was time to depart, Joseph packed Gabriel with supplies for their journey. Finally, Joseph assisted Mary as she sat on the donkey. "I do dread this journey to Bethlehem, but I so appreciate your preparations and this little donkey."

"Bethlehem," thought Gabriel with a start. "That's a three days' journey!" He had never gone so far, especially with a passenger aboard. He wasn't sure he could make it; but as they began their trek from Nazareth to Bethlehem, he was about to find out.

When you've been told all your life that you're worthless, you begin to believe it. For Gabriel, the hardest part of the journey was struggling with self-doubt. Within the first five miles he was stopping periodically to rest and even tried to lay down. But Joseph's words of encouragement and firm grip on the rope attached to his harness convinced him to keep going.

Just as darkness was creeping down the hillsides, they came to a place located by a stream where several families were camping. There they chose to spend the night. Joseph helped Mary down from Gabriel's back and then led the little donkey to the stream to get a well-deserved drink.

Another traveler looked over at Joseph and his donkey. "Ah, good sir. If you don't mind me saying so, that's a peculiar looking animal you have there." Gabriel shuddered at the man's comment.

"Looks can be deceiving, my friend," said Joseph. "He's a fine and reliable animal." Gabriel turned to look at Joseph curiously, for it had been the first words of praise that Gabriel had ever received.

As Joseph and Mary awoke with the first light of day, they found an alert little animal who actually seemed anxious to be back on the road. As Joseph helped Mary onto Gabriel, he had to comment, "My, Gabriel sure has spirit this morning."

The remainder of the journey was far different for Gabriel. No longer was he consumed with concerns about himself. Instead, he was focused on his precious cargo—the sweet and kind woman and her unborn child. When he came to a rock or rut in the road,

Gabriel was careful to walk around it. Yes, Gabriel was tired; but that didn't matter to him anymore.

Late on the third day, Joseph led Gabriel into the village of Bethlehem. They wandered through the village until they came to a house. Joseph knocked and immediately was greeted by smiling faces. "Joseph, Mary, you're here."

"It's good to be here," replied Joseph. "The journey has been a long one."

As Joseph was helping Mary down and unloading the donkey, Joseph's kinsman explained, "Family members arrived before you and the guest room is full. You and Mary will stay with us. Our home is your home." Gabriel was secured outside as Joseph and Mary disappeared inside the house.

It was dark and stars filled the sky when Joseph's kinsman came out to lead the animals inside for the night. Along with a cow and a sheep, Gabriel was led into the stable attached to the home where he, along with the other animals, received fresh hay and water. Gabriel looked into the living area of the house and noticed the warm light produced by a number of oil lamps. As his eyes adjusted to the light, he couldn't quite believe what he was seeing. Something lying in the manger was gently moving. As he drew nearer he spied Mary, leaning over the manger and humming a sweet song. A baby? A baby! The baby! It was Mary and Joseph's baby whom he had help carry to Bethlehem. Mary looked over and spied curious Gabriel gazing at the baby. She smiled gently and said, "Gabriel, meet Jesus."

Keeping as close to the baby as he could, Gabriel bedded down for the night. He wasn't sure how a donkey could keep watch over a baby, but he would do his part. Heavy eyes soon closed and he was fast asleep.

Gabriel was awakened by a commotion in the house. There were strange men gathered around Mary and the baby. They were on their knees as if in prayer. Gabriel overheard them telling of angels and a bright light. "They told us that this child is the Savior, the Messiah, the Son of God."

Gabriel felt flushed. His heart began to pound. Unaware, he had served the Son of God. He hadn't done much; but he had done his best. A warmth filled Gabriel's heart. He had lived up to his name. He was Gabriel, the hero of God.

The day would come when the child would grow into a man. The day would arrive when he would choose to ride into Jerusalem to shouts of Hosanna, proclaiming his identity as the Savior of the world. And, perhaps on that day, he would remember a little donkey who traveled the hard road from Nazareth to Bethlehem. For he did not choose that day to ride on a mighty horse as would high officials and great warriors. Nor did he decide upon a majestic camel as did the wise men who came from the east to Bethlehem. No, he entered Jerusalem as King of kings and Lord of lords, seated upon a donkey.

Questions for Reflection and Discussion:

1. From the beginning of its life, the little donkey is devalued because of his appearance. When and how have you learned that appearances can be deceiving?

2. What is the relationship between how we see ourselves and what we are able to accomplish?

3. Who are the people in your life that have helped you realize your value to God and others?

4. When the Evergreens Whisper

The first flakes of December snow fell gently from the sky and silently touched down on the bows of the evergreens. The tree farm seemed an endless sea of pines and spruces carefully planted in straight rows. A gentle chilly breeze moved in from the north and played among the evergreens; and if you listened carefully, you could imagine the evergreens whispering to one another.

The little Scotch pine at the end of one long row of trees listened carefully as a great blue spruce whispered to the other trees about the upcoming celebration of the birthday of the King.

"Christmas is the greatest of holidays," it announced, "when the birth of the King of glory is celebrated with royal splendor."

The little pine wondered what this great king was like. Surely a king must have been born in regal majesty. The little pine imagined a great palace, a bejeweled crib, plush carpets, and many servants.

"The greatest honor any evergreen tree can receive," declared the great spruce, "is to be chosen to celebrate the royal birth as a Christmas tree. And the most exalted honor," continued the spruce, "is to be chosen as the Christmas tree to decorate city hall."

The little pine imagined itself decorated with candles and tinsel, glass balls and velvet bows, all in honor of the King's birthday. Wouldn't it be splendid? How beautiful it would look and feel. Just thinking about it made its needles stand on end.

"But how do they move the Christmas tree from the nursery to city hall and to the homes?" inquired the curious little pine.

"Well, that's the hard part," answered the great blue spruce. "The tree must be cut free from its roots if it is to serve as a Christmas tree."

"Oh my," moaned the little pine, "doesn't that hurt terribly?"

"Not really," answered the spruce. "I have been told that a sharp saw cuts almost painlessly; but an ax can inflict some pain. Still, it is worth a little pain to serve the King on his birthday."

As the first light of morning broke on the horizon, the evergreens began to whisper, for this was the day the official Christmas tree for city hall was to be chosen. Each tree wondered out loud, "Could it be me?" But when the little Scotch pine uttered the question, "Could I be the one this year?" it heard a chorus of rude chuckles.

"You?" responded the great blue spruce. "Have you ever looked at yourself? You are small and misshapen. You have two tops, not one. Your trunk is crooked and your backside is nearly bare. Who would want you as a Christmas tree?"

The little pine was shocked. No, it hadn't ever looked at itself. Sure, it sensed that it was always looking up at the other trees; and yes, it had noticed that its shadow revealed not one, but two tops; and it had felt a draft many a time from its backside. But did this mean it would never be chosen to hold a place of honor as the city Christmas tree?

A few hours later the word began to spread among the trees that the mayor and several other officials had arrived at the tree farm. By now the ground was covered with crisp snow that crunched under foot as they approached. The sound of footsteps grew louder and louder. The closer they got, the more excited the little pine became. The anticipation was almost too much to bear. Suddenly, the sound of footsteps stopped. A voice of authority said to the others, "This one will do quite nicely." The voice was near. Very near. Had the little Scotch pine been chosen after all to decorate the city hall in celebration of the King's birth? But no, the mayor and city officials were standing in front of the great blue spruce. As the great spruce fell to the ground, so fell the hopes of the little pine to hold the place of honor at city hall.

In the days to come the nursery became a very busy place. The sound of footsteps and the rhythmic singing of the saw could be heard often up and down the rows of trees. Each time the sound of feet drew near to the little Scotch pine, it would strain to straighten its crooked trunk and hold up its limbs; and each time the footsteps would pass by and stop in front of another. The little pine noticed that many of its neighbors had disappeared, chosen to decorate some home in honor of the King's birth. As the days passed and Christmas approached, the little pine became quite discouraged. It began to ignore the footsteps. Day after day its discouragement was fed by rejection. Maybe the great spruce had been right. It would never be chosen as a Christmas tree.

The day before Christmas arrived with little fanfare in the tree farm. By now, the trees that would be Christmas trees had already been chosen and decorated. The little pine had been left behind to weather the wind and taste the bitterness of broken dreams.

It was nearly sundown when the little pine was startled by approaching footsteps. The familiar voice of the owner of the tree farm spoke to a man, a woman and several small children. "This is the one. I can let you have it for, oh . . . I should know better, but . . . it's yours for ten bucks."

"But I only have five dollars to spend," replied the man.

"Friend," answered the owner with a hint of superiority in his voice, "this is a business, not a charity. But it is Christmas Eve and, since I like you folks, it's yours for five bucks."

Could this be? Had the little Scotch pine actually been chosen after all to hold the place of honor in some home in celebration of the King's birthday? How would it be decorated? Would they use splendid glass balls or fine red velvet bows? Would it decorate a great bay window for all to see and admire? Would there be mounds of finely wrapped presents placed around its trunk?

Just then it dawned on the little pine that it was about to face the pain of the saw or, even worse, the ax. The little pine tried to prepare itself, but it was frightened. It tensed for a moment and then heard a strange sound. It was not the cutting of a saw or chopping of an ax. It was the sound of a shovel biting into fresh earth. The little pine felt the dirt around its roots loosen as the man pulled on its trunk. Soon it was free from the ground. Old burlap filled with dirt was wrapped around its roots and it was loaded into the back of a pickup truck. Despite the cold, the oldest child joined the tree in the bed of the truck.

The ride for the little pine was an exciting one. As it gazed at one splendid home after another, it could not help but hope that one of those lovely homes would be the place that it would decorate. Before long the lights of the city were in the distance and the darkness of the country was all around. Finally, the truck turned off onto a bumpy dirt road. After several minutes of bouncing, the pickup truck pulled into a long driveway and stopped at a weary old farmhouse.

As the little pine was carried into the living room, it was struck by the plainness of its surroundings. The house was clean, but everything was so shabby. The hard, cold wooden floors were in need of a good coat of varnish. The furniture was thread-bare and the curtains were tattered. There was nothing splendid about these surroundings. Surely, any hope of fine glass ornaments and velvet ribbons was out of the question. As it turned out, the little pine was right. The father carried in an old washtub and placed the burlap covered roots of the little pine into it. The children quickly began to hang homemade paper ornaments, a string of popcorn, and another of cranberries, to decorate the little pine. At the top was placed a misshapen foil star. A few candles were added and the family of five stood back and admired their work.

They actually seemed pleased with the little pine, but it was not at all pleased. After all, this was not the splendid honor promised by the great blue spruce. There were no glass balls or velvet ribbons, no bay windows or sense of being beautiful.

It was then that the mother began to unpack and arrange a number of little figures under the tree. The strange figures were chipped and faded. There was a man, a woman, a little baby lying on a bed of straw, and a few animals. The figures seemed to represent some poor family of considerable importance, but who could they be?

When the mother had finished arranging the figures, she called the children to gather around as she told them a story. She spoke of a woman who was about to have a baby and of her husband who accompanied her to a city called Bethlehem. She described the hard trip over rough roads. When they had arrived, there was no room in the inn, and so they settled with staying in the barn. It was there that her child, her firstborn son, was delivered. Angels sang and shepherds worshipped. It was a curious story.

That's when the little pine got the shock of its life. Lifting the figure of the child sleeping on the straw, she declared, "The baby Jesus, the King of glory, was born that first Christmas night."

This was the king? questioned the little pine. This was the royal infant whose birth it was celebrating? But he was not born in a palace, laid in a bejeweled crib, or surrounded by servants. He was bedded on straw and surrounded by animals. How could this be the King of glory? How could this be the Son of the Creator?

"Mommy," inquired the youngest, "how come baby Jesus was born into a poor family?"

"I guess," chimed in the father who was sitting in a chair in the corner, "God wanted us to know how much he loves people like us—plain, ordinary, everyday folks."

"Do you think the baby Jesus would like our Christmas tree?" asked the oldest child.

"The baby Jesus would think it's the most beautiful tree in all the world," her mother replied warmly.

The most beautiful tree in all the world! They were talking about the little pine. The great blue spruce on the tree farm had laughed at the dreams of the little pine; but here in this simple home, it was the most beautiful tree in the world decorated with paper ornaments and a foil star in honor of the King of glory.

When the first signs of spring appeared and the ground white with snow melted into a gentle green, the little pine was carried out to a clearing and planted in the warm earth. There, growing in its new environment, the little pine had the honor of sheltering many nests of birds and families of rabbits. But the greatest honor and privilege of all was the Christmas it served as the family Christmas tree.

Many years have passed since the little pine was carried into the old farmhouse. Several generations have come and gone since the children decorated the little pine as a Christmas tree, and the little pine is no more. Where there once was a clearing, there is now a grove of evergreens—Scotch pines to be exact. On cold December nights, as the first flakes of winter snow descend upon their branches and the wind blows ever so gently from the north, you can almost imagine that the evergreens are whispering. They whisper of a glorious King born to poor parents, a Creator who especially loves all who are humble, and the great honor of being chosen to adorn paper snowflakes and foil stars to the glory of the King.

Questions for Reflection and Discussion

1. The great blue spruce tells the little Scotch pine, "The greatest honor any evergreen tree can receive is to be chosen to celebrate the royal birth as a Christmas tree; and the most exalted honor is to be chosen as the Christmas tree to decorate city hall." What is the difference between honor and personal recognition?

2. How do you respond to comments by those whom you respect that your dreams are unrealistic? How do you deal with disappointment when your dreams do turn out to be unrealistic?

3. What are the differences between how the great blue spruce and little Scotch pine honor the King of glory?

5. The Night the Candles Weep

Emily, like all children, was excited about Christmas. She was three years old, turning four in January. When asked how old she was, she would proudly respond, "Free, but almost this many"—holding up four fingers.

In the next room, Emily's parents were making a big decision—a big decision for the parents of a preschooler that is. Her mother was convinced that this was the year to take Emily to the Christmas Eve candlelight service at the church. After all, she went to Sunday school almost every Sunday and was learning at preschool how to sit still and stay occupied, at least for a time. Emily's father was not sure.

Steve warned, "You know what happened at your sister's wedding last month. You had to take her out and then missed half the ceremony."

"Steve," responded Jean, "I want Emily to learn what Christmas is all about. With all the ads on television and hype about getting presents, we have to do something to help her understand that Christmas is about giving, not getting. Anyway, your dad will be there. You know how good he is with her. He'll keep Emily occupied."

"Sure he will," retorted Steve. "He's as much a kid as she is."

"Come on," encouraged Jean. "Let's go tell Emily what she's going to be doing tonight."

That evening Steve, Jean, Emily, and her grandpa arrived early at the church. Steve insisted that if they weren't early, they might get stuck in the front row. As they entered the sanctuary it was less than half full. The family chose a pew near the back to provide an easy escape to the nursery.

As they walked toward their seats, a smiling woman handed each of them a candle slipped through a cardboard circle. Emily took the candle, looked strangely at the woman, and then gazed at her surroundings. Her eyes were wide as she beheld the sanctuary dimly lit by candles. She liked the pretty red bows on the wreaths and the twinkle lights in the garland, but she was particularly taken with a huge Christmas tree covered with decorations prepared by the children of the Sunday school.

Emily tugged at her grandfather's sleeve. "Look Grandpa, there's mine!"

"Your what dear?" inquired her grandfather.

"My decoration. The one I made in Sunday school for the tree. See it? It's there, almost on top."

From that distance all the children's decorations looked pretty much the same, but Grandpa didn't let on concerning his confusion. "Oh yes, I see it," he exclaimed. "It's the most beautiful angel I've ever seen."

"Grandpa, it's not an angel. It's a star!" responded Emily indignantly.

"Oh, of course it is," chuckled Grandpa.

Emily tried to keep herself occupied waiting for the service to start, but that is a tall order for a little girl on Christmas Eve. She looked at the pretty picture on the bulletin cover and decided it needed some work. She pulled out a pew pencil and added several details. Only Emily knew what they were supposed to be. Having finished her artwork, she again picked up the candle the smiling woman had given her and noticed something strange. The candle had a cardboard skirt around it. Emily had seen candles before, but she had never seen one wearing a skirt. Why would the church want to put skirts on candles?

Her curiosity got the best of her and, tugging again at Grandpa's sleeve, she asked, "Grandpa, why do candles wear skirts?"

Thinking his granddaughter was telling a joke, he responded dutifully, "I don't know. Why?"

"No Grandpa," complained Emily. "See, my candle has a skirt on it. How come?"

"Oh, that's not a skirt," he answered. "That's a tear-catcher." Convinced his little granddaughter had had enough of hard pews, he took her by the hand and said, "Come on, let's go for a walk and I'll tell you a story."

Wandering down the hall, Grandpa found a pleasant room with comfortable furniture. Lifting Emily into his lap, he began his story: "Now, let me tell you why candles wear tear-catchers on Christmas Eve.

"Long ago a little candle was made along with many other candles in a great candle factory. But this was no ordinary factory. The candles made there were to be used in churches to glorify God. Their light would tell people of the light of God. The candle was packed in a large box with other candles and delivered to a lovely little church, much like this one."

"Did the candle like being in church?" asked Emily.

"Hold on," warned Grandpa. "You're getting ahead of me. Now one day a man just about my age opened the box and, with his large, rough hands, carefully took out fourteen candles. Our little candle was one of those candles. The man said to them, 'You are indeed fortunate candles, for this Sunday you will have the great privilege of showing forth your light in the sanctuary to tell all of the light of our Lord God, the Creator of the universe.' The man took the candles and placed them in two beautiful candelabras. The little candle was very excited. It was told by the other candles that this was why it had been made. Its light would glorify God and bless the people of God when they came to worship on Sunday.

"Sunday morning came and, as the music started, two children dressed in robes came forward and began to light the candles. Our little candle was the last one to be lit because it was at the top. It stood straight and proud as its wick was lit.

"Now, for a candle, it is a disgrace to drip; especially if you are a candle on a candelabra whose light is to glorify God. Well, our little candle used all its strength to hold back the wax that had melted at its center. Though several small breezes nearly blew a drop of wax down its side, it refused to budge, but held fast to the liquid wax.

"The little candle loved every moment of the service. Beautiful music was mixed with beautiful words. It hoped that the service would go on forever; but all too soon the two children were back, this time extinguishing the flame of each candle. All the people who had come to see the light of the candle got up and left. The lights were turned on and it was over. Was that all? Was this why the little candle had been made? How it yearned for the children to light its wick again that its light might glorify the Creator.

"'When will they light us again?' it asked the candle next to it.

"'Oh, so you don't know. We are only privileged to light the sanctuary one time,' the candle next to it answered knowingly but sadly.

"'But what will become of us?' begged the little candle.

"'We will see,' responded its neighbor.

"And indeed, they did see. Monday morning came and with it the man with the rough hands who had first placed the candles in the candelabras. He removed each candle and carried them all to a little room behind the sanctuary. He pulled out an old knife and began to trim the candles. First the wax at the top was cut even and then the wick was trimmed. The little candle was afraid it would hurt but was surprised to discover that it did not. Though it was somewhat shorter than before, the little candle felt almost brand new. It hoped that maybe this meant it would again fill the candelabra, but the little candle was instead placed in a large box with many other trimmed candles.

"'What happens to us now?' inquired the little candle of its new neighbors.

"'We do not know,' they responded in a tone that was most discouraging. 'We have been in this box for a long time. Each week more candles are added, but none are taken out.'

"The little candle waited day after day, week after week, hoping to be used to again glorify the Lord God with its light. Each

Monday the lid of the box in which it was stored would open, the man would add more candles, and then he would close the box again. After several months of this, the little candle had lost all hope of lighting the sanctuary again.

"Then one day the lid of the box was lifted off and the little candle was removed along with all its neighbors. One by one the neatly trimmed candles were taken and a paper circle was placed around each."

"The skirt!" exclaimed Emily.

"No," answered Grandpa. "The tear-catcher. That night," he continued, "the sanctuary began to fill with people. The little candle could see that something special was happening, for the sanctuary was decorated with greenery and bows. The little candle was disappointed that the candelabras in the front were already filled with candles that were glowing bright and proud. Wondering anxiously what part it was to play in the festivities, the little candle felt itself lifted from the box where it had been placed earlier and handed to someone."

"Was it a little girl?" inquired Emily.

"Indeed, it was," Grandpa said agreeably. "The little girl took the candle and held it in her warm hands. The little candle worried that it might bend as she played with it. She fiddled with the paper circle, which the little candle found very annoying. Then she began to pick at its wax, just like you're doing now."

"Oh, I'm sorry little candle," apologized Emily.

"That's okay, I'm sure. Anyway, as the music began, the little candle's heart swelled. The music was even more beautiful than before and the people all seemed to sing with love in their hearts. But still, the little candle remained unlit. Someone in a long robe stood in the pulpit and began to read from a book he called the word of God. The little candle listened intently as the story was told of God's Son being born as a little baby in Bethlehem. The story was the most beautiful the little candle had ever heard and it was pleased to have had the opportunity to hear it.

"It was then that the little candle realized what this church service was all about. This was a birthday celebration for the Son of God. The light of the candles that day were to glorify the Son of God and tell of his light to the world. Still, the little candle remained unlit.

"The service was nearly over, and the little candle had given up all hope of shining its light to glorify the Son of God that night. That's when all the lights were turned off and the loveliest song the little candle had ever heard began. The sanctuary slowly became brighter and brighter. Suddenly someone appeared with a lighted candle in hand and lit the candle of the person at the end of the pew. One by one, the people passed the flame from one candle to another until it was finally passed to its own wick. The little girl held the candle very carefully and looked with wonder all around her at the many lit candles. The little candle stood tall and true, thrilled that it once more was able to light the sanctuary, this time at the birthday celebration of the Son of God. The little candle made a promise to itself that, like before, it would not lose even a drop of wax.

"That's when everyone began to sing, and with them, the little girl. 'Silent night, holy night. All is calm, all is bright.' The song was more beautiful than any it had ever heard before and the girl's voice sounded to the little candle like that of an angel. As she sang, something happened to the little candle. It was so happy and so moved by the beauty of the night that it wept first one, and then another, and then another drop of wax.

"'Oh no,' thought the little candle. 'My hot wax will burn the little angel and she will drop me.' But no, the little paper circle, the tear-catcher, caught the drops of wax. Because you see, Emily, on this beautiful night, when little girls sing 'Silent Night,' the candles are moved to weep."

Grandpa noticed that music had begun in the sanctuary. He silently took Emily by the hand and led her back to their seats. She carried in her other hand the candle that had been the subject of Grandpa's story. As the service began, Emily wondered if her candle would weep that night. She listened to the reading from the Bible, she tried to keep her eyes closed and hands folded during the prayer, she even attempted to sing some of the hymns she didn't know, but all the time she wondered if her candle would weep that night.

When the minister finally finished his sermon, music began that sounded familiar to Emily. It was her favorite Christmas carol, "Silent Night." As the organ began to play, some people came forward holding candles. The minister lit their candles, and as they walked down the center aisle, they lit the candles of others. Soon Grandpa was leaning down with a lit candle in hand to light Emily's candle. As the sanctuary grew brighter from the light of the candles, the organ music swelled and everyone began to sing, "Silent night, holy night; all is calm, all is bright."

Emily gazed at her candle, the flame dancing at each breath as she too sang the words she knew or could understand. Sweetly she sang, and though her small voice could barely be heard amidst such a great number of people, it surely must have been heard in heaven. And then it happened. Even while she sang, a tiny drop of wax rolled down the side of her candle onto the paper circle. Then another and another and another.

"Look Grandpa," she exclaimed. "My candle. It's weeping, just like the one in the story." But when she looked up at her grandfather, she saw a tear slowly making its way down his cheek. For you see, on that holy night when the little angels sing, the candles weep, and sometimes, so do grandpas.

Questions for Reflection and Discussion

1. Do you believe it is important for children to be present in worship? Why or why not?

2. How does Grandpa's story help Emily to participate more fully in the worship service? How can we help children to become more fully engaged in worship?

3. How can seeing the world through the eyes of children provide us with insight?

At the Manger

6. A Night for Dreaming

The streets of Nazareth were quiet, but the light in the window of Joseph's carpenter shop revealed that, for at least one citizen, the day's work was not yet done. Joseph's hands ran carefully over every inch of the new cradle he was creating. There would be no ragged edge or sharp splinters to cause discomfort for the child when he was born. Joseph's care would see to it. Joseph was not sure if it was the sawdust or the late hour, but it was becoming harder and harder to keep his eyes open. Still, with Mary now approaching her ninth month, he knew there was little time to complete this labor of love. A little more sanding and, perhaps, he would reward himself with sleep.

Joseph was nearly finished for the night when he heard a gentle tapping on the door. Joseph slowly approached the door and spoke firmly, "Who is there?"

Joseph feared a drunken Roman soldier might be on the prowl and think a lighted window late at night served as an invitation for a fight.

"Joseph, it's me. Eli," answered a familiar voice.

Joseph unbolted the door and was relieved to see the face of his friend. "What brings you out so late at night, Eli?" inquired Joseph.

"What keeps you up so late?" retorted Eli.

"I'm trying to finish the cradle before the baby is born," responded Joseph as he stepped aside so Eli could behold his creation.

"Joseph, you never cease to amaze me," gasped Eli. "It is magnificent. I doubt there is a carpenter your equal anywhere in Israel."

Joseph thanked Eli for the compliment, but then interrupted, "You didn't tell me why you are out so late."

"I couldn't sleep and I saw the light on in your shop. I have a big decision weighing on my mind and I hoped, maybe, you would help me make it."

Joseph nodded and said, "Go on."

"I was visited earlier this evening by Reuben," continued Eli. "A small group of men from the area have banded together as Zealots. Reuben asked me to join with them."

"Eli, no!" objected Joseph.

"Joseph, please hear me out," pleaded Eli. "He told me the time has come for us to make the Romans pay for taking our land and terrorizing our people. He placed a cold steel dagger in my hand and asked me to imagine thrusting it between the ribs of one of those Roman soldiers in the streets. Strangely, it felt good. It felt right. I can't sit idly by and allow this abomination to go on any longer."

"Eli," warned Joseph, "the Zealots will be the downfall of our people. They have rejected the way of God for the way of vengeance. They appeal to the worst in people—their anger and bitterness and fear. Do you really think shedding the blood of a few Roman soldiers is going to change anything? It will make the resolve of Rome even firmer and many more innocent Jews may pay for the sins of a few."

Eli glared at Joseph. Somehow, he expected him to share his vision of revolution. Angered by Joseph's accusations, he blurted out, "What do you know? You, whose life is so simple and full of blessing. You with your solid business and lovely young wife and firstborn on the way. What do you know of the anger and bitterness I feel?"

Joseph looked confused. Eli had moved to Nazareth three years ago, but he had said very little about his background. Joseph knew he had come from Caesarea, but little else. "Tell me," Joseph said.

Eli began his tale of pain and sorrow. "When I was just nine years old and living in Caesarea, a group of drunken Roman soldiers came to our door one night. They spoke rudely to my father and said they were coming in to spend the night. One soldier spotted my mother and said perhaps he would spend the night with her. My father's face turned red and he stepped into the doorway to block their entry. He told them to be gone before there was trouble. Suddenly a sword was drawn and my father lay before me, his life running red on the floor. The soldiers quickly disappeared. We complained to the Roman governor, but nothing was ever done. They told the elders that the guilty soldier had been dealt with, but we all knew it was a lie to calm the people. Suddenly I became the man of the house, a boy expected to act like a man. My mother was never the same after that. Her kind and warm disposition gave way to quiet grief. So often, as I looked in her eyes, I sensed that her very soul died that day along with my father. Though many years passed, she never really got over it. She died still grieving. When I laid her to rest, I decided I could not tolerate Caesarea another day. I packed my few possessions and moved here to Nazareth; but I vowed that if the opportunity ever came to avenge my father's death and mother's grief, I would take full advantage of it. So you see, Joseph, my anger and my bitterness are justified. Surely the Lord God would bless any act of vengeance I might take against the Roman swine."

The pained look on Joseph's face told Eli that he understood and cared. Joseph remained silent for a moment and then uttered, "My friend, I am sorry. So sorry."

Eli's eyes filled with tears and he answered, "I know, but do you understand why I must do this?"

Joseph did not respond at first. His eyes fell to the ground. It was clear he was pondering deep and troubling thoughts. Finally, he broke the silence. "Eli, I'm going to tell you something I swore to myself I would never tell another living soul. You must solemnly promise not to repeat a word of this to anyone; for if you did, they surely would not understand."

Eli looked confused, but pledged nonetheless, "I promise."

Joseph leaned forward on the stool on which he was sitting. "Eli, my life is blessed as you said earlier, but it has been anything but simple. It was in the early spring when Mary broke to me the news that she was with child. I knew the child could not be mine since I had never known her."

"Joseph, no," interrupted Eli. "How could Mary have done such a thing to you? Why didn't you expose her for the harlot she is?"

"Silence!" shouted Joseph. Eli fell back on his stool as though a blow had been struck against him. "Do not speak of things you do not understand, cannot understand."

"Joseph, I'm sorry," gasped Eli. "I did not mean to offend."

Joseph composed himself and went on with his story. "I guess I should not have shouted at you; for I had some of the very same thoughts. I was the one who was angry and bitter at such news. My hopes and dreams for the future were dashed before my very eyes. My heart was broken. I had a hundred questions to ask, but I said nothing. I just turned from her and walked away. I sat in my home a full day and night pondering what I must do. I prayed that God would show me the way; but I grew only more confused. Finally, I determined that, though I had every right to expose her, I could not. I decided that I would write her a certificate of divorce and dismiss her quietly. I knew tongues would wag and people would condemn me for leaving Mary with a child presumably fathered by me, but it was a risk I knew I must take for her sake. That's when it happened Eli."

"What?" asked Eli. "What happened?"

"I had a dream," shared Joseph. "Anger is exhausting and before the sun had completely disappeared in the west, I fell asleep. My sleep was restless and I tossed in fits from side to side."

"I know restlessness in sleep, too," commented Eli.

"Then I suddenly sensed a great calmness coming over me and in the midst of my dream, I saw an angel."

Eli's eyes grew big. He leaned forward to ask a question, but then fell back on the stool without uttering a word.

6. A Night for Dreaming

"The angel spoke words to me that were strange and wonderful. I can still remember them word for word. 'Joseph, son of David, do not be afraid to take Mary as your wife, for the child conceived in her is from the Holy Spirit. She will bear a son, and you are to name him Jesus, for he will save his people from their sins.'"[1]

Eli waited for more, but there was no more. Finally, Eli broke the silence with a question. "What does this mean?"

"It means," said Joseph, "that God is about to keep a promise made long ago, a promise that the Messiah will come. And that very child is the one who will soon sleep in this crib. Don't you see, Eli? This is how God responds to Roman soldiers who shed innocent blood and Zealots who respond by shedding more blood. God comes into the world as a little child to save us."

Eli sat silently, pondering this strange and wonderful story he had just been told. After a few moments Joseph broke the silence. "Good night, my friend. It will be dawn before we know it and another day's labor without a little rest is unthinkable to me right now."

"Oh, yes," replied Eli awkwardly as he got to his feet. "Thank you for listening to me."

"And thank you for listening to me," replied Joseph.

Eli stepped out into the dark street and turned the corner toward his home. In the darkness he did not see the figure staggering toward him.

"Oh," said Eli with a start, "excuse me." Looking up he beheld a Roman soldier obviously filled with too much wine returning from some late-night revelry. Eli's heart started to pound as he felt the dagger still tucked secretly in his girdle. He began to reach for it as the light of a lamp in a nearby window faintly illuminated the soldier's face. He beheld the countenance of a young man, possibly still in his teens. He thought of his sharp steel blade piercing the heart of this youth. He thought of the mother who would be grieved. He pictured a young wife and possibly children who could be left alone. The young soldier looked confusedly at Eli, mumbled

1. Matt 1:20b–21.

41

something, and then staggered on down the street. Eli continued to his home shaking with emotion.

Exhausted, Eli fell into his bed. That night there was not the customary tossing and turning. There were no sudden starts that so often caused him to sit up in bed. On this night, Eli did what he had not done for many years. Eli dreamed. He dreamed of a world where there were no wives left widowed and children left orphaned. He dreamed of a world where there were neither swords of injustice nor daggers of vengeance. He dreamed of a world of peace and goodwill. And he dreamed of a little child whose coming promised all these things.

Questions for Reflection and Discussion

1. Eli was obsessed with a desire for vengeance based upon an experience of gross injustice during his childhood. What does Eli most need to hear from those who care about him?

2. Why did Eli let go of his obsession for vengeance when faced with the opportunity to shed the blood of his perceived enemy?

3. What difference does it make in our lives when we believe the promises of God?

7. When a Child Leads

A young warrior crept slowly, silently, toward the house, sword and shield in hand. With the quickness of a lion, he burst through the door swinging the sword overhead. "Prepare to die, cursed Philistine," he shouted.

"Nathan, how many times must I tell you, not in the house." A young woman was setting the table for supper. Her stern expression was betrayed by her smiling eyes.

"Yes, Mother," moaned Nathan as he shuffled back outside. Nathan was eight years old, the only child of Jacob and Sarah. He lived with his parents in the beautiful foothills of Mt. Carmel in Galilee. There his father grew some of the finest grapes in all of Israel. The sweet wine made from his grapes was much sought after, and, as a result, Nathan's family was better off than most.

Every eight-year-old boy has his hero and Nathan's was King David. Maybe this was because, as his grandfather use to tell him, David's blood flowed through his veins. Nathan's father was of the tribe of Judah and traced his lineage back to David. Nathan's eyes lit up every time the scrolls of Samuel recounting the deeds of King David were read in the synagogue.

Nathan spied another Philistine masquerading as a tree seedling and went about hacking it with his sword and protecting himself from attack with the shield. His sword and shield were a gift from his grandfather. It was the last gift he had made for Nathan before his death. The sword was crafted from hardwood and, except for its color, could almost pass for a miniature version of the real thing. The shield was of goat skin stretched over a wooden frame. They were his prized possessions.

Nathan stopped his attack long enough to notice the sun was going down. His stomach confirmed that it was past suppertime. Nathan entered the house again.

"Mother, why is Father late tonight?"

"He said there was an important meeting in town."

In a matter of moments, a tall man with a few highlights of gray accenting his hair and beard entered the house.

"Those cursed Romans," he growled. "They make a decree, and everyone is expected to drop what they are doing, pull up their families, and go wander across the countryside."

"What happened?" Sarah inquired.

"The emperor has decreed that everyone is to return to the city of his ancestors to be counted. What do they expect me to do? Grape vines don't dress themselves. There's so much to be done!" he complained.

"King David wouldn't let then get away with this," bragged Nathan, "and when his offspring, the Messiah comes, he'll show those Romans just like David showed the Philistines."

Jacob's face grew pale and his eyes opened wide. He knelt down, grasping his son's shoulders, and began speaking firmly in a hushed voice. "You must never talk that way. There are Roman soldiers everywhere. If they heard you speak like that, they could arrest me for sedition."

Nathan had no idea what sedition was or why his words so displeased his father, but looking quite guilty, he slowly made his way to his place at the table and sat down quietly. Soon his parents joined him. After a prayer of thanksgiving to God, the food was passed. Jacob, noting his son's unusually somber mood, sought to soften the effects of his stern warning.

"Nathan, do you know what the Roman decree means?" asked Jacob. Nathan, looking down, shook his head no. "It means," Jacob paused for effect, "we are going to Bethlehem."

"Really?" Nathan responded, his face lighting up. "The city of David? We're really going?"

"As soon as I can make arrangements," Jacob responded, pleased at his son's delight. "You must help your mother prepare for the long trip, for I have much work to do to get ready, and," Jacob continued, "you may take along your money you earned helping me last summer. On the way home we will stop at the marketplace in Jerusalem."

The time preparing for the journey seemed like an eternity to young Nathan. He would start a job for his mother, but she would find him off daydreaming, his task half-finished. Patiently she admonished him to get back to work; but it was hard for Sarah to be angry with her son. He had talked so often of going to Bethlehem. He had been there once; but he was much too young at the time to remember. Now he would finally see the home of his hero.

On the day of departure, the family rose early and were on the road leading south. It would be a long three-day journey. Still the miles went quickly for Nathan as he fought imaginary foes along the road with his sword. Once, as they were passed by a Roman regiment, a soldier snatched Nathan's sword from his hand.

"Please, "Jacob pleaded, "it's only a toy given him by his grandfather."

The soldier scowled and then, throwing the sword at Jacob's feet, responded, "A sword in the hand of a Jew is never a toy."

The remainder of the day's journey was uneventful, and the family chose a pleasant place to camp as the sun was setting. As Sarah unpacked the food for the evening meal, Nathan helped his father build a fire. Soon another pair of weary travelers settled down nearby. A kind looking man helped his young wife down from their donkey. It was obvious she was going to have a baby. Sarah looked at Jacob and commented, "And you complain of inconvenience. Can you imagine how they must feel?"

Jacob had to nod in agreement.

"Jacob," continued Sarah, "take them a skin of your wine. You have brought more than enough, and I know they will enjoy it." Smiling, Jacob unloaded a skin from his donkey and walked toward the couple. Jacob was invited to sit and soon the men were engrossed in conversation. Jacob learned that his fellow travelers were also descended from David and were headed for Bethlehem. He and his wife were from Nazareth and assumed their child would be born while in Bethlehem. Nathan walked over and sat silently at his father's feet.

The kind-faced man looked down at Jacob, ruffled his hair, and said, "I hope I have a handsome boy just like you."

Sarah had already approached the young mother-to-be and invited her to sit by the fire. She asked them to join her family for dinner and the young woman agreed with expressions of gratitude. Following dinner, the long day's journey began to tell on the weary travelers and sleep prevailed before long.

Morning found the travelers refreshed and Nathan awoke to a flurry of activity. While the men packed up camp, the women prepared a light breakfast. Nathan watched the young mother-to-be through sleepy eyes. So much was happening and yet there was a strange calm about her. Although he didn't know why, looking at her made him feel good inside. Slowly Nathan got up, stretched, growled a yawn, and approached his mother. The cool morning air sparked his appetite and he sat by the embers of the fire with bread and a little sweet wine.

"We would be pleased to travel with you," offered Jacob to his fellow travelers.

"That is most kind of you," replied the man sincerely, "but our pace is rather slow. We would only delay you. We will be fine."

After a brief farewell, Jacob, Sarah, and Nathan returned to the road leading south. Nathan found the day's journey less appealing and was ready to stop and camp by mid-afternoon. That night Nathan lay looking up at the stars, wondering where the young couple they had met were camping and whether anyone was helping them this night.

The final day's journey was a mixture of excitement and impatience for Nathan. Every few miles he would look up at his father and asked, "Are we almost there?"

"Soon, Nathan," Jacob would respond. "Soon."

Sarah would chuckle at this; and when Nathan showed unusual patience during one stretch of the journey, she brought a smile to Jacob's weary face by asking, "Jacob, are we almost there?"

It was late afternoon as they entered the little village of Bethlehem, already crowded with visitors. Jacob had arranged with a cousin who lived in Bethlehem to stay in his guestroom and set about unpacking their few possessions from the donkey. Meanwhile Nathan, eyes wide with fascination, took in every detail of his surroundings. There was a certain magic Nathan could feel in this place. He could almost imagine King David strolling down the street, welcoming visitors. Nathan held his sword and shield firmly in hand as he imagined David inviting Nathan to join his men.

"Well, are you going to stand there daydreaming the rest of the day or would you like to see Bethlehem?" Jacob asked, smiling.

Sarah extended her hand to her son and they strolled down the street together. Bethlehem was a rather small village with a tiny marketplace and several hundred inhabitants, but to Nathan every house and street had a tale to tell. Much too soon for Nathan's liking the sky began to darken and lamplight in windows signaled that it was time to return to their guestroom. Nathan protested that he was much too excited to go to bed, but the long journey quickly caught up with him and he was dreaming of adventures only eight-year-old boys understand.

Nathan was awakened by some kind of commotion outside. It was quite dark, but voices and flickering lamps told the boy that something was going on. Silently Nathan slipped from his bed, careful not to disturb his parents. He grabbed his sword and shield and stepped outside into the cool night air. Down the street he could see a group of men who had gathered at a house. They seemed quite excited about something. As he drew near, he could hear them talking about strange and wonderful things—angels, a Messiah, and a baby lying in a manger.

"He must be the Promised One," said one man.

"I'm sure of it," said another. "Our time of waiting is over."

Nathan took a few steps forward and peeked through the open door of the house. The warm lamplight revealed a man and woman looking at something. As he poked his head in the door, he was surprised to see the friendly couple he had met on the road. As the new mother's eyes met those of Nathan, she smiled as though she recognized him. Motioning him into the room, Nathan slowly approached. There in the manger lay a tiny new baby sound asleep. Nathan looked on with wonder in his eyes. No words were spoken, but as Nathan looked up at the man, he ruffled Nathan's hair as he had before and smiled warmly.

It was then that a voice behind Nathan broke the silence: "The wolf shall live with the lamb, and the leopard shall lie down with the kid, and the calf and the lion and the fatling together, and a little child shall lead them."[1] It was Nathan's father, quoting from the prophet Isaiah. His mother knelt down and put her arms around her son. Together they looked at a scene they were sure they would never forget.

Slowly, Nathan moved closer, his toy sword and shield in hand. He looked intently at the child and placed his beloved possessions at the foot of the manger. As the family left the home, Nathan looked up at his father. "Father, do you think he is the Messiah?" he asked.

"We can hope so," he replied. "We can hope so."

The stay in Bethlehem was far too brief for Nathan's liking and the family was soon headed north again. The distance between Bethlehem and Jerusalem was not far, but it seemed so to a young boy excited to see the big city. The crowds of people and the enormity of the walled city were breathtaking to Nathan. As they approached the noise of the marketplace, Nathan tugged on Jacob's sleeve. "Father, may I have my money now?" Jacob opened his purse and counted out seven coins into Nathan's waiting hand. Nathan closed his hand tightly as his eyes began to search the many wares the merchants had to offer. As they walked through the narrow streets of the market, Nathan suddenly stopped, his eyes firmly fixed on an item. There on a merchant's table was an olive wood carving of King David, sword and shield raised high in victory. Nathan turned, looking for his father's approval.

1. Isa 11:6.

"Go ahead, Son. See if you can get it for a fair price," Jacob counseled.

It was then that Nathan spied her—a young woman sitting in the shadows, an infant in her arms. The woman was dressed in a ragged, patched robe and her thin face revealed her poverty. Nathan stood silently, looking at her and then slowly approached. The woman looked up at the boy, a startled, curious expression on her face. Nathan took the coins in his hand and pressed them into the hand of the young mother.

As Nathan turned, he noticed tears in the eyes of his parents. "And a little child shall lead them," uttered Sarah.

Questions for Reflection and Discussion

1. What do children see that we sometimes miss? Why?

2. What do you think it means when Nathan lays his sword and shield at the foot of the manger? What might be an equivalent response for you to the wonder and mystery of the incarnation?

3. Nathan does not give the woman one coin or some coins. He gives her everything he has. What might this say about our response to God's gift in Jesus?

8. A Soldier's Story

Marcus stood at attention, his eyes constantly scanning the crowd, his right hand firmly gripping his sword. Marcus was a Roman soldier and proud of it. The son of a Roman soldier, Marcus could still remember when, at the age of ten, a messenger came with the tragic news that his father would not return home. It was then he had committed himself to follow in his father's footsteps. Now a man in his early twenties, Marcus was about to become a father himself.

Despite his pride in his work, Marcus was torn by his responsibilities back home in Tarsus. When he was called away, his wife was great with child. For all he knew, she could have given birth by now. Would everything go all right? Would the baby be healthy? Would his wife face any complications?

Marcus might not have wrestled so with these questions if he had been called away to do battle with an enemy. He was a brave soldier and remained focused in the midst of every conflict. But why did the emperor find it necessary to call a census of the empire just when he was about to experience the birth of his first child? For days, Marcus had stood guard at one of the booths in a village called Bethlehem, where Roman officials enrolled the people. It was not enough that Caesar Augustus should call for an enrollment of all who lived in the empire, but he also insisted that each man and his family go to the town or city of their origin for enrollment. The normally quiet village of Bethlehem was bustling with travelers whose lives had been as disrupted as his own.

It might seem strange to see Roman soldiers on high alert in such a tranquil village as Bethlehem, but Marcus and his fellow soldiers had been warned to expect trouble. Bethlehem was the city of David, the place of origin of Israel's greatest king. It did not seem to matter to the people that he had been dead for a thousand years. The Jews believed that one of his descendants would come to reign as a powerful king. They called him Messiah—the Anointed One. It might be expected that such anticipation would have faded away over the centuries, but it only seemed to grow.

This Jewish hope in a messiah might have seemed harmless if it was not for the shadowy terrorists who called themselves Zealots. They were the worst kind of enemy. They moved in stealth. They blended into crowds. Their daggers were sharp and their deeds were swift and lethal. Worst of all, they hated Romans. They believed they were doing God's work and will as they thrust their knives into their next victims. Occasional reports of Roman soldiers found slain in dark alleys and quiet streets within Israel served as warnings to all in uniform to be on alert at all times.

Still, unlike most of his fellow soldiers, Marcus did not despise the Jews. Marcus had been raised in Tarsus, a prominent city in which a fair number of Jewish families had lived. They were respectful and respectable neighbors. Marcus had even become friends with a Jewish family who always warmly welcomed him into their home. After the death of his father, Samuel had taken him under his wing. When he took his own sons hunting, he would always invite Marcus along. As Marcus grew into a teenager, he became fascinated by the religious traditions of his Jewish friends. Marcus had found the worship of the Roman gods and goddesses somewhat foolish and scandalous. The deities he was supposed to appease seemed like little more than immortal beings with very human qualities. But his Jewish neighbors spoke of one God whose mystery and majesty fascinated Marcus. He dared not let on to his Roman friends that he had taken an interest in the Jewish God; but the more he heard of and experienced their faith, the more drawn he was to them. It was from Samuel's lips that he first heard the word "messiah." Many religions speak of heroes who will come and lead their people in conquest of the enemy, but this Messiah was different. Samuel spoke of one who would bring God's goodness to the whole world. He talked, not of bloodshed and spoils, but of justice and peace.

Marcus was startled by a voice behind him calling his name. Turning around, he stood face to face with his commander.

"It's good to see you so alert at your post, Marcus. I need two of my best men to guard the census documents. I have selected you and Antonio. We are concerned that these Zealots might come at night and try to destroy the records. Caesar would not be pleased if we failed to complete his order to enroll the citizens of this village. Stay awake and investigate any suspicious activity. I'll reward the two of you with a good rest and extra rations."

"Yes sir," snapped the two young soldiers.

The large number of people that had filled the marketplace had diminished to but a handful as the sun dropped low in the sky. The Roman officials had closed their records and safely tucked them away. They expected that, with the rising of the sun in the morning, the lines of those to be enrolled would again form.

The sky was a pale blue-gray and the first stars were faintly twinkling when two shadowy figures entered the village near where the two soldiers stood. "Keep an eye on those two," Antonio said quietly. As the figures drew nearer, Marcus could see that the late arrivals posed no threat. A Jewish man and his wife were apparently arriving for the census and it was clear the woman would be delivering a child any day now.

"Oh, great," said Antonio just loud enough for the strangers to hear. "Just what we need. More Jews to count."

Without responding to Antonio, Marcus approached the couple. As he looked at the young woman, he could imagine his own dear wife and his anticipated child. The couple seemed startled and apprehensive at first at the sight of an advancing Roman soldier.

Joseph stepped in front of Mary and spoke up. "Please sir, we are here for the enrollment. We have traveled from Nazareth in Galilee and have made arrangements to stay with relatives. We plan to enroll in the morning."

The warm, relaxed expression on the soldier's face eased Joseph's concern. Marcus responded, "Then I will not detain you. Go and seek shelter quickly. It appears you will soon be a father."

Mary looked up at the soldier and smiled shyly, her face revealing the exhaustion that was setting in after a long trip in her condition.

"Go," motioned Marcus. "Go quickly. It will soon be dark."

As it grew later and the sky grew darker, the light of extinguished lamps was replaced by a canopy of stars. Marcus looked up in fascination at the countless number of heavenly bodies and tried to imagine a Being capable of creating such splendor and beauty. His mind was drawn, not to the gods and goddesses of his ancestors, but to the strange and wonderful God of Israel. Could all that lay before him be the handiwork of the one the Jews called the Creator of heaven and earth?

As the last lamps that illuminated the windows throughout the village were extinguished, the silence of the village signaled that the little town of Bethlehem was falling off to sleep. There was a sense of peace in this place that was palpable. Marcus drifted to thoughts of his childhood and his young wife about to have a baby.

Marcus didn't know how much time had passed, but the silence was suddenly broken by Antonio's voice. "What is that?" Marcus looked as Antonio pointed to a group of figures entering from the hillside into the village. The figures moved as one, apparently searching for something. They disappeared around a corner and were gone.

"I don't like this," said Marcus. "People don't travel this late at night unless they are up to no good. Our commander warned us about this. You stay here and I'll go investigate. If I need help, I'll come back for you."

"Be careful," warned Antonio as Marcus moved in the direction taken by the group of men.

Marcus gripped his sword firmly as he slowly advanced toward the narrow street into which the men had disappeared. As he continued, he noticed a faint light ahead. Drawing closer, he observed the group of men for which he was looking. He quietly moved forward, remaining in the shadows in order to avoid detection. Could these be the Zealots about whom he had been warned? He was just about to return to Antonio to alert him when he heard the word spoken.

"Messiah."

They were telling someone that divine messengers had announced to them the birth of a new king. The Messiah! They entered a home and, before long, came out again rejoicing as though they were leaving a celebration. Clearly these were not terrorists moving in stealth. From their dress, they appeared to be shepherds. But what were shepherds doing in the village late at night? Shouldn't they be out on the hillsides tending their flocks and protecting them from predators?

Marcus stepped back into a doorway to remain undetected as the joyous group passed by. He then continued down the alley to investigate what the men had been doing. He approached the door that was still ajar. He pushed on the door and could see the couple who had arrived at dusk apparently settling in for the night. The man was making a bed for his wife who was placing a child on straw in a manger.

Startled by the figure at the door, the man arose and stepped forward nervously. "May I help you?" he asked awkwardly.

Marcus took a step forward, forgetting how intimidating he could look in his uniform in the flickering light of a lamp. "I'm sorry to have startled you. I see your little one has arrived. Is there anything you need?"

Joseph stared back at the soldier, wearing a look of surprise. "No, but thank you," he uttered.

"Messiah," whispered Marcus.

Joseph's eyes grew large and he glanced nervously at the baby lying in the manger.

"I overheard the men who were here. They spoke of a Messiah and then knelt before your son."

Joseph froze, not knowing what would come next. Would he call other soldiers? Would they be arrested? Was the child in danger?

The soldier came closer and knelt by the child. "By now, I may be a father too. I was also forced to come to Bethlehem at an inconvenient time. My wife was close to delivering our firstborn in Tarsus when I was called here. I hope my firstborn is as beautiful as yours."

The young soldier took his purse from his belt, loosened the strings, shook out a silver coin, and handed it to Joseph. "A gift for a newborn king," he said with a smile.

Marcus got to his feet and bid goodnight to the family. As he stepped from the light into the shadow of night, he whispered, "I hope he is the Messiah."

"Is everything all right?" inquired Antonio as Marcus returned to his post.

"Nothing to worry about. A young woman gave birth in a house up the street," answered Marcus.

"Just what the world needs! Another Jewish brat," chuckled Antonio.

"Just what the world needs," repeated Marcus as he gazed into a star-filled sky.

Questions for Reflection and Discussion

1. How can personal experiences with people different from us dispel stereotyping?

2. How do common experiences help us to empathize with others?

3. What have you learned from other expressions of the church or other religions that has aided you in your faith journey?

9. The Messenger

The elders gathered by the fire as was their custom each evening. The night was clear, the sky faded from a deep blue to gray to black, and stars cut through the gathering darkness with their heavenly light. The flickering glow in nearby windows signaled the lighting of oil lamps to counter the growing darkness. The village of Bethlehem was settling in for the evening.

"Well, where is he?" asked old Enoch impatiently. "I do not want to retire for the night without hearing a little news from Jerusalem."

"Nor do I," responded Isaac, "But I'm sure he will be here. Brother Enoch, with your many years of leadership in our village, you have no doubt learned patience with the young."

Enoch's furrowed brow softened. Just the tiniest hint of a smile forced the corners of his mouth upward. He stroked his gray beard several times and shook his head. Enoch liked Isaac. Isaac always had a way of stating his mind, yet without showing disrespect for those whose leadership had stood the test of time.

"Yes, Isaac, you are right," Enoch replied. "I know how to be patient when I must. If I want to hear news from Jerusalem, I will be patient this night. As you say, he will be here." The other elders seemed to relax at old Enoch's words.

The one for whom they were waiting was known as the Messenger. No one was sure of his age, though most guessed he was in his early twenties. Rumor had it that his mother had died in childbirth and he had been abandoned by his father when it became known that he was not like other children. He could not learn to read and had difficulty answering simple questions. As he grew into manhood, he had come from his home village to Bethlehem. He had arrived in Bethlehem in the presence of merchants who had hired him to do menial tasks; but the merchants had slipped away one night, abandoning the young man in a strange place.

It was Isaac who found him one morning, sleeping in an alley. The young man appeared weak, hungry, and frightened. Isaac had quickly noticed that the man was simple and unable to care for himself. He had fed the man, given him an old cloak Isaac no longer wore, allowed him to stay in his vacant guest room, and gave him a few chores to do to earn his keep. Yet even the simplest tasks had seemed to confuse the young man. Still, there was something about him that fascinated Isaac. Though he struggled to formulate an idea of his own, he had the extraordinary ability to remember and repeat the words of others. He could recall long stories or lengthy instructions word for word, without error.

One evening Isaac had brought the young man to the gathering of village elders. The simple young fellow sat staring off into the distance, apparently oblivious to the conversations that took place around the fire. But when Isaac asked him to share with the others what had been said, much to the shock of those gathered around the fire, he repeated their conversation verbatim.

Isaac spoke to the other elders. "I have an idea. I believe this simple one with the extraordinary memory is a blessing from God." Isaac reminded the elders how isolated they often felt, though they were not far from Jerusalem. News from the holy city seemed to take forever to travel south to their little village. "Let us make this young man our messenger," he had suggested. Isaac had proposed that they send the young man to Jerusalem, one day on for travel and reporting, one day off for rest. It went without saying that he would observe the sabbath each week. For his labors Isaac suggested that the Messenger be provided with a day's worth of bread, a skin of fresh goat's milk, and a coin to cover any travel expenses to and from Jerusalem. The other elders appeared slow to agree until old Enoch had sealed the deal by standing and declaring, "So it will be. Let us see what this young marvel can do."

Added Enoch, "If nothing else, this could be quite entertaining."

This brought smiles and a lot of head bobbing from the others.

That's how the Messenger had begun his regular journeys from Bethlehem to Jerusalem. In the early morning light, he could be seen walking up the road that led north. Arriving in the city, he made his way to the temple area. Once there, he wandered from place to place, group to group, listening to their conversations. The simple facial expression of the Messenger led others to dismiss his presence and before long he was even able to eavesdrop on the conversations of officials and priests. By mid-afternoon, the Messenger, his head full of words he did not fully comprehend, began his journey home. Arriving in Bethlehem in the early hours of evening, he would seek out the place where the elders gathered. At their prompting, he would tell of matters both important and irrelevant. Some evenings the stories were of rabbis preaching in the temple courtyard or merchants grumbling that business was slow.

But all the elders remembered with satisfaction the evening the Messenger had revealed to them what appeared to be a plot to drive down the price of their lambs. The priests apparently had been discussing how to increase their profits from the lambs sold in the temple courtyard for sacrifices.

"We will tell those fools in Bethlehem that their lambs are growing inferior in quality and are therefore of lesser value," they said. "They must settle for one-third less or we will threaten to purchase the lambs elsewhere."

The other priests had seemed pleased with the plan. But when the elders of Bethlehem had heard the Messenger repeat the conversation, they took half their lambs and hid them. When the chief steward of the priests had come to Bethlehem to bargain for lambs, he was informed that the flocks had not produced well and a shortage had developed. Instead of selling their lambs for a reduced amount as proposed by the priests, they had demanded and received an extra twenty percent. Memory of such critical inside information compensated for the evenings when the Messenger had nothing of significance to tell. Whether the Messenger brought information of importance or irrelevance, he was provided with his bread, milk, and coin.

The sky was now a deep ebony and the air was turning cool. Even Isaac was growing visibly impatient as the Messenger slowly emerged from the shadows.

"There you are!" exclaimed old Enoch. "What has kept you? It is growing late. Come and tell us the news of the day."

The Messenger stood staring at the group huddled around the fire. Something was different. The expression on his face revealed a mingling of confusion and fear. Isaac got to his feet and approached the Messenger. Taking him by the hand, he gently pulled him toward the group of elders.

"Brother, what is it?" asked Isaac. "What disturbs you? What news do you bring us this night?"

The Messenger looked up at the gathering of elders. He began to speak. "Do not be afraid; for see—I am bringing you good news of great joy for all the people: to you is born this day in the city of David a Savior, who is the Messiah, the Lord."[1]

The group sat in silence for a moment, the look of confusion on every face. Old Enoch slowly arose to his feet and the others quickly followed suit. Enoch stepped forward toward the young man, his staff in hand to compensate for tired knees. "Little bother," exclaimed Enoch, "who spoke these words? Was it the high priest? Was it one of the great rabbis? Was it . . . was it a prophet of God?"

The Messenger's head dropped and his eyes were directed toward his feet. He mumbled something inaudible. Enoch reached out and lifted his chin. He leaned in and asked again, "Who told you this?"

"Shepherds," uttered the Messenger.

"Shepherds?" questioned Enoch. "Shepherds in Jerusalem? What would shepherds be doing in the holy city? Why would shepherds be speaking about the Messiah's coming? Where did you hear these shepherds speaking?"

1. Luke 2:10b–11.

The Messenger's mouth puckered up in a sort of pout. He shuffled his feet in the dust. Finally, he answered, "Bethlehem."

"In Bethlehem!" exclaimed one of the other elders. "Do you mean that you did not travel to Jerusalem today!" His voice began to grow louder as he walked toward the Messenger. "Do you mean to tell me that you come with news from our own village and tell us fantastic tales from the lips of shepherds?"

"This will be a sign for you," continued the Messenger, "you will find a child wrapped in bands of cloth and lying in a manger."[2]

Old Enoch shook his head. "What utter nonsense," he groaned. "For this I submitted my aching bones to the dampness of the night. Let us retire and hope on the morrow that the next time our young brother will have the good sense to venture beyond Bethlehem in search of news."

"And what of his bread and skin of milk?" interrupted Isaac.

"One only receives payment for a job completed," complained the agitated elder.

Isaac quickly responded, "This simple brother must eat and drink like all of us."

"Yes, brother Isaac, you are quite right." With these words, Enoch held out to the Messenger the bag of bread and skin of milk. He reached out, took them, and then watched as the elders dispersed to their homes.

But Isaac remained. He was not sure why, but he remained. The Messenger looked at Isaac and began to speak again. "This will be a sign for you: you will find a child wrapped in bands of cloth and lying in a manger."[3]

"I know where he is," said the Messenger, a smile breaking across his face.

"You know where who is?" Asked Isaac.

"The child," he answered. "I know where he is."

And without another word, the Messenger disappeared down a dark street. Turning a corner and then another, the Messenger stopped in front of a house. The faint glow of an oil lamp signaled

2. Luke 2:12.
3. Luke 2:12.

that those inside were still awake. The Messenger approached the door and gently knocked. A man slowly cracked the door and, upon seeing a familiar face, swung the door wide. The Messenger entered and the man motioned him to come closer. In the arms of the mother was a tiny baby, fast asleep.

"Here," said the Messenger. "For you."

He held out the bag of bread and skin of milk. The father stepped forward and reached out, taking the offering and pulling out the bread. He said a blessing, took a piece of bread, handed a piece to his wife, and then to the generous visitor.

"Thank you," he said, "and God bless you."

"Yes," responded the Messenger. "God bless me," and he smiled broadly.

A noise behind the Messenger startled him and he turned to see a figure standing at the still-open door. The figure stepped forward and the light of the lamp illuminated the face of Isaac. Isaac stood still, staring at a scene he could not quite comprehend. The Messenger walked toward Isaac, took him by the hand, and gently pulled him forward. Pointing to the baby, now lying on a bed of straw in the manger, the Messenger proclaimed, "Do not be afraid; for see—I am bringing you good news of great joy for all the people: to you is born this day in the city of David a Savior, who is the Messiah, the Lord."[4]

Questions for Reflection and Discussion

1. What qualities in Isaac do you find admirable? Why?

2. The Messenger is a savant with autistic tendencies. How do you respond to Isaac's arrangement between the Messenger and the village elders?

3. Isaac is the only village elder to see the newborn Messiah. What does Isaac do that the other elders do not?

4. Luke 2:10b–11.

10. The Shepherd Rabbi

The sun had nearly set as dark shadows crept up the sides of the rolling hills surrounding Bethlehem. A young shepherd sat on a great rock facing the sunset, bathed in orange and red light. His lips moved silently as he recited to himself the great prophecies concerning the coming of Messiah. He knew them by heart.

"A shoot shall come out from the stump of Jesse, and a branch shall grow out of his roots. The spirit of the Lord shall rest on him . . ."[1]

"For a child has been born for us, a son given to us; authority rests on his shoulders; and he is named Wonderful Counselor, Mighty God, Everlasting Father, Prince of Peace.[2]

"But you, O Bethlehem Ephrathah, who are one of the little clans of Judah, from you shall come forth for me one who is to rule Israel, whose origin is from of old, from ancient days."[3]

David, a young man barely twenty years of age, was more at home with his dreams than with his daily routine as a shepherd. He fancied himself a student of the Law, the Prophets and the Writings, much to the displeasure of his older brother, Jephthah. David was often sneaking away to stand in the shadows of the synagogue in Bethlehem and listen to this or that rabbi visiting from nearby Jerusalem, addressing the local scribes and Pharisees. David loved to hear the rabbis teach and longed to sit at their feet and converse

1. Isa 11:1–2a.
2. Isa 9:6.
3. Mic 5:2.

with them; but he knew he could not, for he was but a shepherd, as they often reminded him.

There was a time when David identified himself as a shepherd with great pride. He could remember sitting around the fire with the other shepherds as his father told tales of noble King David.

"Good King David wandered these very hills as a boy, tending his flock and singing psalms of praise to God," he would say. Then he would look intently at his younger son and declare, "Be proud of your namesake, David, for you are a descendent of the greatest king of Israel, and from his seed will come Messiah."

But as David grew older, he found some of the villagers were less impressed than his father with his heritage and role as a shepherd. Especially frustrating was his rivalry with a young Pharisee named Reuben. David had tried on several occasions to enter into discussions in the village on the law and prophets, but Reuben would break off such discussion when David approached.

"When shepherds begin to practice the ritual purity required in the law of Moses as we do," he would say to his companions, "perhaps we will discuss theology with them."

His worst nightmare came true, not in Bethlehem, but in Jerusalem, the holy city. A particularly noteworthy rabbi was to speak in the temple courtyard while David and his brother were there selling unblemished lambs for sacrifices at the temple. When David heard of it, he determined that he must attend. Changing into his best robe, he joined the gathering of students of the law at the feet of the rabbi. He was discussing the promised Messiah, a subject about which David felt some confidence. He arose to his feet and asked the rabbi which prophet spoke most clearly of the signs of Messiah's coming. The rabbi looked approvingly at young David and responded, "And you are a student of which teacher?" At that, all eyes turned to David and, to his horror, one pair of eyes belonged to Reuben. Reuben arrogantly arose to his feet and, drawing near to the rabbi, said in a voice just loud enough for all to hear, "Teacher, he is no student of the law. He is a shepherd from Bethlehem."

David's stomach burned each time he thought of that day. He knew the law. He could quote the prophets as well, no better, than Reuben. Still, he was dismissed as nothing more than an ignorant shepherd. Sometimes humiliation seemed worse than death.

David's thoughts were broken by the voice of Jephthah. "Are you off in your dreamworld again? I have rounded up all the sheep into the sheepfold, no thanks to you. Where is your mind, little brother?"

"Jephthah, I'm sorry, but I was meant for better things than tending sheep," he responded with a touch of bitterness in his voice.

"David, you have to stop this," demanded his brother impatiently. "Our grandfather was a shepherd; our father was a shepherd; and we are shepherds. That is the way it is and as it should be. Your words dishonor our father's memory!"

"Jephthah, I would never do that," responded David apologetically.

"Then begin to take pride in your work again," answered his brother. "Remember father's stories of King David? He taught us to hold our heads up and tend the flock even as we would serve the Lord."

"But Jephthah, we are not respected," David argued. "I spend every spare moment memorizing the Scriptures. I know the Law better than many of the students of the Law. But they will not discuss the Scriptures with me. They will not even acknowledge my presence."

"Little brother, all you lack is self-respect," responded Jephthah harshly. "You seek approval from people who will buy our lambs to sacrifice to God at the temple, but refuse to sit at the same table with us. Brother, what are you searching for?"

"I don't know," admitted David, "but I know this much—I haven't found it yet."

"Well, I'm tired," remarked Jephthah. "You take the first watch. I rounded up the sheep alone so you could slip into that dreamworld of yours. Now you can dream on while I get some sleep. Watch out for predators."

In the quiet, David's eyes pierced the darkness dimly broken at times by the flickering of the fire. The voices of distant shepherds could be heard from time to time. The crackling of the flames was a welcome sound and the warmth of the fire made for good company. David pulled his cloak up tightly around himself and sunk deeply into thought. He wondered about the promises of old. A Messiah, a great king descended from David—when would he come and what difference would it make?

Suddenly David's contemplation was shattered by an experience the shepherds would always have difficulty describing. There was a figure in the midst of a bright light. The figure said they should not be afraid and that he was bringing good news. He told the shepherds that a Savior had been born in Bethlehem who was the Messiah. And he provided them with a sign of this holy birth— they would find a baby wrapped in swaddling clothes and bedded in a manger. It was then that the light grew even brighter and a host of figures sang, "Glory to God in the highest heaven, and on earth peace among those whom he favors."[4]

As quickly and unexpectedly as it began, it ended. David found that he was no longer seated, but on his knees. He looked around to find Jephthah sprawled out on the ground, his mouth hanging open in amazement. Soon the silence was broken by the chatter of shepherds talking excitedly. David heard someone say, "Could this mean Messiah has come?"

Messiah? thought David. *Messiah has come and we are invited?*

David thought of all the people of importance who must surely have been informed of this great moment for Israel. Priests from Jerusalem, great rabbis, the leading scribes and Pharisees— surely they had all been invited. All those important people, and he was invited!

"David," Jephthah interrupted. "Come! We are going into Jerusalem to see the sign that God has promised."

David and Jephthah walked briskly in the direction of the other shepherds who had already headed toward the village. As they walked, David gazed with wonder into a star-filled sky and

4. Luke 2:14.

imagined the surprise on Reuben's face when he too arrived to honor the newborn king.

As they caught up to the others, one of shepherds exclaimed, "Young David, you know the prophets better than any of us. Tell us their words of promise about the One whose birth was announced to us."

David recited one passage after another of the promises for a Messiah. He spoke with passion and authority of what God would do through this anointed one.

As they entered the village, the shepherds divided up to search for the one whose holy birth had been shared with them in the form of a heavenly invitation. Every street, every alley was assigned for careful exploration. David and Jephthah knocked on several doors, hoping to gain some clue as to the whereabouts of the newborn Messiah. None had heard anything about a special birth.

"Jephthah, why does no one know of this extraordinary event?" asked David, confused by the normalcy of sleepy little Bethlehem. "Did we see what we saw and hear what we heard? Were we asleep and dreaming?"

Before Jephthah could answer, another shepherd came running around the corner shouting, "We have found him! We have found him! Come quickly!"

The brothers hurried down the street and turned a corner. There was a gathering of people outside a rather ordinary house, not unlike the one David's family lived in. Carefully straightening his robe as best he could, he prepared to join the honored guests at this regal visitation.

David took a deep breath and entered the house. The scene before him was illumined by several small oil lamps. There in one corner, a mother who looked younger than David was tending to her newborn. The father stood to one side, gazing with satisfaction upon the child. Clearly, these were peasants, dressed simply, their child wrapped in swaddling clothes and bedded down in a straw-filled manger.

It was then that his eyes scanned the guests—only himself and the other shepherds. No priests, no scribes, no Pharisees. No Reuben. Slowly he approached his brother and asked in barely a whisper, "Where are they?"

"Where are who?" replied Jephthah.

"Where are all the honored guests?" continued David.

"I guess you're looking at them," Jephthah answered with a smile.

"But what does this mean?" asked David, flushed with confusion.

"It means we shepherds matter. It means shepherds have been invited by God to behold the Messiah. God has honored us with the privilege of being the first visitors of this holy child."

When it was his turn, David slowly stepped forward and looked to the father for his approval. At his nod, David knelt by the manger and gazed at the child. David felt a firm hand on his shoulder and looked up to see Jephthah gazing down at him. They exchanged a look that spoke of family and love and faith. That night, David not only found the Messiah. He discovered his dignity again.

Many years have passed since that strange and wonderful night, and many things have happened in Bethlehem. Not long after that night, foreigners from the east visited the village, looking for the child. Shortly after their visit, the family—parents and child—quietly left Bethlehem and seemed to disappear. Then there was that day David wished he could forget, when Roman soldiers and weeping families tore a hole in the heart of his people. To this day, a Roman soldier dares not walk alone on the streets of Bethlehem. Just last year a plague stole away far too many of his neighbors, among them his brother Jephthah. And now a rumor has spread of a mysterious prophet who reminds many of Elijah and who is baptizing people in the Jordan.

With stiffening joints and painful knees, David still makes his way into the fields and joins with the younger shepherds of the village as they watch over the sheep. David continues to study the Scriptures, memorizing the words of life and sharing them with all who will listen. Reuben, now a leading Pharisee and influential elder in the village, mockingly nicknames David the Shepherd Rabbi, a name that amuses David and which is adopted by the shepherds who love and respect him. It is not unusual to see the younger shepherds seated with David around a fire on the hillsides surrounding Bethlehem as he tells stories of a young shepherd named David who became the greatest king of Israel. He quotes the words of the prophets that had brought hope and inspiration to God's people for generations. He speaks passionately about the power of the Messiah, who will bring peace and justice, not just to Israel, but to the whole world. And, before he finishes each night, a young shepherd will always say, "Rabbi, tell us again of the night when the angels sang and the shepherds of Bethlehem knelt before the newborn Savior."

Questions for Discussion and Reflection

1. In his rivalry with Reuben, with what personal issues is young David wrestling?

2. At the manger, what do you think the look between David and Jephthah meant?

3. There is a clear difference between the perspectives and actions of young David and old David. What are those differences? What do you think brought about those changes?

A Homespun Christmas

11. The Miracle of the Creche

"Joe, they're starting," Janice shouted from the living room.

"Whose starting what?" asked Joe.

"The cars, they're starting to line up to see the creche," Jan replied.

Joe walked in the living room and joined his wife at the window. It happened every year like clockwork. Two weeks before Christmas, peopled traveled from near and far to see the famous creche on the lawn of the Presbyterian Church in Parkview, Indiana.

The people of Parkview liked to call themselves a suburb of Indianapolis; but, in reality, Parkview was just one of many insignificant little towns that dotted the Indiana landscape. Most people would have never heard of Parkview if it hadn't been for the creche. The hand-carved and painted life-size wooden creche was the creation of Doc Leonard, who over the years had added new pieces until the nativity scene nearly filled the front lawn of the church. Now retired, Doc would gladly chat with anyone who wanted to know about his famous creche. "It was on the cover of the December 1979, issue of *Life Magazine*," he proudly told visitors. "They've got the cover framed and hanging in the narthex of the Presbyterian Church if you'd like to see it," he would add. "Feel free to stop by any Sunday morning." As a member of the church's Evangelism Committee, Doc was constantly trying to land new members for the church.

Joe and Janice looked out the window as the line of cars grew longer. Living just a block and a half from the church, they faced a traffic jam each evening from the first Sunday in December until Christmas Day.

"I'd find all of this annoying," commented Joe, "if it wasn't so beautiful."

"Joe, let's go see it," Jan said. Joe didn't need to be asked twice. He grabbed his jacket and helped Janice on with her coat. "Do you think Doc has added another character?" she asked.

"Well, there's only one way to tell," answered Joe as he opened the front door. The crisp December air met them as they stepped outside and started down the sidewalk. Other neighbors had the same idea and a steady stream of pedestrians mirrored the line of automobiles heading in the same direction.

As Joe and Janice reached the church lawn, they stopped and joined the crowd that was already forming. Floodlights illuminated the rough-hewn stable and the characters of the nativity.

"They're so lifelike," Jan exclaimed. "You almost expect them to move."

"Evenin' folks." It was Doc Leonard. "How do you like my newest addition to the creche? It's my final contribution. As far as I'm concerned, it's now complete."

There were Mary, Joseph, the baby Jesus, the angel, the shepherds, the wise men, a sheep, a camel, even a donkey, but nothing new that they could notice.

Doc pointed toward the holy family. "The little lamb lying near the manger," Doc said. "I think that little lamb makes the scene complete."

"It's breathtaking," gasped Janice. "I never tire of seeing it."

As snow began to fall, Joe and Janice made their way through the crowd and headed for home. As they started up the front walk, their teenage son Jack came sailing out the door.

"Whoa, son. Where are you headed in such a hurry?" asked Joe.

"Oh, hi, Dad. Hi, Mom. There's a basketball game tonight. I'm supposed to take pictures. The guys are gonna pick me up on the corner. Gotta hurry."

"But Jack," Jan shouted as he headed down the sidewalk, "what about the creche?"

"I've seen it before, Mom," he shouted back and disappeared around the corner.

"These kids," lamented Janice, "they're always in such a big hurry."

"Oh, let him go," Joe said. "Boys need to keep busy. It keeps them out of trouble."

Joe and Jan were startled from a deep sleep by sirens and flashing lights. Joe went to the window as a fire truck, followed by a police car, sped by. Joe looked at the clock. It was nearly three in the morning. He assured Jan he would check things out as he pulled on his pants and a sweatshirt. He met Jack in the upstairs hallway.

"Dad," moaned Jack, half-asleep, "what's going on?"

"I don't know," Joe responded, heading down the stairs, "but I'm going to find out."

Joe slipped on his boots, unlocked the front door, turned the knob, and was out the door in a matter of seconds. The cold air and gently falling snow were mixed with the acrid smell of smoke and ash.

Joe looked down the street in the direction of the smoke and flashing lights. "Oh no. Not the church," he whispered to himself.

Joe started to run in the direction of the excitement. As he drew nearer, he could see the source of the smoke and smell. The lovely creche and its life-sized figures were still smoldering as a fire fighter doused them with water.

Recognizing the fire chief, he quickly approached him. "Steve, what happened?" gasped Joe.

"As best we can figure, vandals," answered Steve. "Someone doused everything with gasoline and lit it like a torch. There's not much left but some charred wood and ashes. It's a shame, Joe. A real shame."

73

"Does Doc know?" he asked the chief.

"I don't think so, at least not yet," Steve answered.

"I just called him. He's on his way." The voice came from behind them. Joe turned to see the pastor, Cathy Burman, staring at the charred remains with tears in her eyes. "This is going to break his heart, Joe," she uttered.

Doc hadn't been too keen on Cathy being called as the church's pastor, but nearly eight years had passed since her arrival and the two had developed a mutual respect for one another. One of the loves they shared was for the lovely creche.

The headlights of an automobile moved slowly down the street toward the church. Joe followed it with his eyes until the streetlights revealed its driver. It was Doc. He stopped and slowly stepped from the car, his eyes fixed on the smoldering scene. He walked in disbelief toward what was once his prized gift to the church. Cathy stepped toward him and put her hand on his shoulder.

"Doc, I'm sorry," is all she could say.

Doc Leonard knelt where the manger had been and ran his fingers over the charred remains that once had been the Christ child. Then he picked up the remains of the little lamb he had recently completed, tried to brush away the ashes, then tossed it aside. "They have no respect anymore," he moaned. "They just don't have any respect for anything."

"Who?" asked Cathy.

"Those teenagers. You know who I mean. It had to be them. These kids today. They just don't have any respect."

Cathy tried to reason with Doc, but he was in no mood for a debate. He stood and started in the direction of his car. As he approached Joe, he could see that Doc's eyes were filled with rage.

He spotted Joe and stopped abruptly. "You have a teenage son, right Joe?"

"Yes, but he was in bed when all this . . ."

"No, no," interrupted Doc. "I'm not accusing him of anything. But you ask him. You ask him who did this. I'm sure it will get around school. You have him find out who did this and . . ." Doc's voice drifted off. He hurried toward the car and drove away.

Janice and Jack were just starting down the sidewalk when Joe met them.

"Joe, what's going on? Is it the church?" Jan asked fearfully.

"No, worse," answered Joe. "It's the creche. Someone doused it with gasoline and burned it."

"What? Why? Who would do such a thing?" interrupted Jack. At first Joe didn't answer.

"Does Doc know?" Janice asked. Still no answer.

"What's wrong?" both said in unison.

"Doc was there," began Joe. "He showed up and the pastor tried to comfort him. But he didn't seem to want comfort. He's angry and he's hurt and . . ."

"Yes, go on, Dad," Jack insisted.

"He blames teenagers. He thinks some young people must have done it. He even wants you to be the informant, to find out who did it and tell him."

"Dad, it could have been anyone. It's not fair. He has no right to blame people without any proof."

"Jack, he's just upset," Janice counseled.

"Still, he has no right," protested Jack.

The days leading up to Christmas were not the same in Parkview that year. It wasn't just the absence of the steady stream of traffic everyone had come to expect. A sadness had replaced the twinkle in everyone's eye. It was as though the whole town was suffering from a broken heart. Usually when there was excitement in Parkview, it was the subject of nonstop conversation in the barber shop and diner, but not this time. It almost seemed disrespectful to talk about the tragedy that had befallen the little town.

It was early evening on December 24 as Janice set the table for dinner. This was usually the most festive meal of the year, but somehow no one felt much like celebrating.

"Joe," she called out to the living room, "Jack's supposed to get home soon. Will you check the ham to see if it looks done?"

When Joe didn't answer, Janice went to the living room to see why her request was being ignored. Joe was standing at the front window.

"Jan, what do you make of this?" he asked in the strangest voice.

Jan stepped to his side and peered out the frosty window. To her amazement, a line of cars had formed down the street in the direction of the church.

Without speaking, Joe and Jan grabbed their coats and headed out the door. Scurrying down the street, they stopped in front of the church. The flood lights were on and there before their eyes was the beautiful creche they had loved for so many years. There was Mary done up in various shades of blue. Joseph was dressed in his familiar robe of warm brown. The shepherds, the wise men, the angel, and the babe lying in the manger—they were all there. Others quickly gathered at Joe and Janice's side.

"Joe," whispered Jan, "it's a miracle."

Just then one of the shepherds sneezed.

"No," replied Joe, "I think it's Jack."

The two approached the shepherd who resembled their son. As they drew nearer, they could see that the characters were all teenagers from the local high school. Each was dressed identically with the wooden figures that had made up the famous nativity scene.

"Jack, how did this happen?" Jan asked.

"A bunch of us got together at the high school and we came up with the idea. I asked the ladies guild if they would sew some costumes, and they said they'd be delighted. Only thing is, we asked them to keep it a secret. Pretty good surprise, huh?"

Joe's eyes slowly scanned the scene in amazement. That's when he noticed the Christ child. He walked ever so slowly toward the manger and there lay an exact replica of the wooden figure that had been the crowning glory of the creche.

"Jack, how did this get here?" Joe asked breathlessly.

Jack pointed over to one of the wise men who winked back. "Doc," ask Joe, "is that you?"

"It's me," he answered. "And thanks to these kids, maybe I really am a little wiser."

Parkview, Indiana is no longer known for the famous wooden creche that once donned the cover of *Life Magazine*. Now it is known for the live nativity that is performed each year on the lawn of the Presbyterian church by the teens of the community and a retired doctor who always insists on being one of the wise men.

Questions for Reflection and Discussion

1. How do you tend to respond emotionally to acts of vandalism?

2. What is the link between emotional experiences and the way we judge others?

3. What does Jesus provide in his actions and teachings to guide us in our judgment when emotions run high?

12. An Old-Fashioned Christmas

Gertrude Baker sat at her kitchen table thumbing through an old cookbook. It was the day before Christmas and Gertie, as everyone knew her, hadn't baked a thing. Why should she bother, she thought to herself. No one was coming to eat her cookies or pies, and she sure didn't need an excuse to put on a few more pounds.

Gertie turned the page and stopped. She let out an audible sigh as she rubbed her finger over a page crusty with old bits of cookie dough and stained with a sticky drop of molasses. She brought the cookbook to her nose and could make out the faint aroma of ginger. For as long as Gertie could remember, clear back to childhood days, she had associated Christmas with gingerbread men. She could still remember how her mother would call her into the kitchen each year a few days before Christmas and tie an apron around her waist. She recalled carefully measuring and mixing the ingredients as her mother supervised, giving directions along the way.

"Now remember the rules, Gertrude," she would remind the little apprentice, "dry ingredients first and then wet ones."

Flouring hands, pressing on cookie cutters, carefully lifting the gingery figures to cookie sheets, and decorating the freshly baked cookies were memories she cherished. She had loved the gingerbread ritual so much as a child that she continued it with her own children. Not only her two daughters, but also her son were invited into the kitchen to measure and mix and bake and create. And when the children grew into adults, too busy to join her in the kitchen, she invited her grandchildren to learn the Baker ritual of Christmas gingerbread men. Well, she didn't call them gingerbread men with her granddaughters. They complained that they wanted to make gingerbread women. And so, from that time on, the gingery delicacies were known as gingerbread people.

Gertie was startled from her daydreaming by the ringing of the phone. She lifted the receiver only to hear the voice of Pastor Schultz calling from Charleston. Yes, she had let the florist into the church as he had asked. Yes, the ten red plants were very healthy and brightened up the sanctuary. Yes, she was also looking forward to the candlelight service, but she was sorry it had to be so early this year. Yes, she understood that Pastor Schultz had to get back to Charleston to lead the service at his other church. Following cordial goodbyes, she hung up the receiver and walked back to the table. She closed the cookbook and slipped it on the shelf.

"Maybe next year," she uttered to herself.

She didn't blame her family for not coming to Narrow Ridge, West Virginia for Christmas. After all, they had their own lives. Her eldest daughter, Margaret, had recently become a new grandmother and, of course, she and Charles wanted to be near their new granddaughter in Atlanta. Elizabeth and her family had recently moved to Dallas and were still trying to turn a new house into a home. Robert had just begun a new job in Memphis and had complained to her over the phone that he might even have to work Christmas Day. Her children all had good excuses, but it didn't ease her disappointment.

Still, she thought to herself, *there's more to Christmas than getting together with the family. What did Pastor Schultz say last Sunday? Oh yes,* "Christmas isn't just a holiday, but a holy day."

That made sense to Gertie, and she shifted her focus from disappointment to anticipation of the candlelight service that would be held in the sanctuary at six o'clock.

Narrow Ridge Presbyterian Church was a small-frame building constructed in the mid 1800s. The once prosperous little coal mining community some thirty-five miles from Charleston had provided a solid congregation of as many as 175 members. But after the mine closed, people started moving away. The church went the way of the community until, on Sunday mornings, as few as a dozen people made up the worshipping congregation.

Gertie recalled how hopeful she had been when the new plant opened on this side of Charleston. She heard that the company made parts for computers and some kind of chips you didn't eat. Gertie didn't know anything about computers, but she could see the plant was doing well when developers came to Narrow Ridge to buy up property. Soon heavy machines were clearing vacant houses and contractors were replacing them with fancy new homes that were bought up quickly by people who worked at the plant. Soon new houses filled with young families surrounded the little church. Gertie was certain the little congregation was about to come back to life.

But it didn't happen. Gertie soon discovered that most of the people who worked at the plant weren't local folks. Many of them had moved all the way from California. Gertie had always been suspicious of people who lived in California. She had heard some strange stories about the place, and now that she discovered these people weren't really interested in church, she was convinced the stories were true.

"People from California who don't go to church, making chips you can't eat. It's just not right," she had complained to her friends.

At four-thirty, Gertie heated a little leftover chicken pie in the oven for an early supper. She quickly washed it down with a cup of strong black coffee and set out to get dressed for church. How Gertie loved the Christmas Eve service. She was a bit unhappy that the service had to be so early; but she understood that Pastor Schultz had to get back to First Church in Charleston for his ten o'clock service. Sharing a minister was hard, but it was better than not having one at all. Gertie slipped on her best dress after carefully ironing out a few wrinkles. She combed her hair, slipped on her shoes, groaning a bit as she bent over to tie them, and then pulled on her coat. Opening the door, she couldn't help but notice the new houses across the way sparkling with all kinds of twinkling lights.

"Kind of gaudy," she mumbled under her breath.

She crossed the road and in a matter of moments was opening the front door of the church. She hung her coat in the little narthex and opened a second door into the sanctuary. She was met by the sweet smell of burning wood and a warm "Good evenin', Miss Gertie."

It was Jebediah Anderson, the community handyman and self-appointed custodian firing up the wood burner. The church had an oil furnace, but the thermostat was set just high enough to keep the pipes from freezing. For worship services, the congregation still relied on an old wood-burning stove situated to the left of the pulpit. You could gauge how cold it was in the sanctuary by how far to the front the congregation sat.

"Merry Christmas, Jeb," Gertie said warmly. "I thought I'd come a little early to make sure everything looked okay. Do you think the poinsettias are in the right place?"

"Yes, ma'am," responded Jeb. "You've got a special way with arranging flowers."

The creaking of the sanctuary door announced that Betty May, the pianist, had arrived. She greeted everyone, slid onto the piano bench, and ran through the music for the evening. Gertie was grateful for the Christmas music.

Betty May wasn't halfway through the second song when Pastor Shultz entered the sanctuary, papers in one hand and his robe draped over the other arm.

"Good evening all," he warmly greeted everyone.

"Evenin', Pastor," responded Gertie. Betty May was on the second verse of "Hark the Herald Angels Sing" and let a brief nod suffice for her greeting.

"Pastor, do you think it's warm enough?" asked Jeb.

"Perfect as always," Pastor Schultz answered.

Before long the sound of wind and something similar to rice hitting the windows provided the first clue of what was to come that night. Fred and Marcie Wilson were the first members of the congregation to arrive for the service. Fred's beard was tinged with ice.

"Fred and Marcie, what's it doing out there?" inquired Pastor Schultz.

"Looks like an ice storm, Pastor," Fred responded. "Was listening to the weather before we came over. Seems a cold front dropped farther south than expected. Weatherman over in Charleston said it could get a lot worse. I'm glad we live just a few houses down. I'd hate to have to drive in this stuff."

Pastor Schultz looked worried. He suddenly was much more concerned with the thirty-five-mile drive he had ahead of him than the worship service he was about to lead in thirty minutes. As the clicking sounds at the windows became more pronounced, Betty May stopped her piano playing and went to the window.

"Lands sake," she blurted out. "Everything's covered in ice. How are me and my old cane gonna get back home?"

Pastor Schultz looked at his watch. It was five minutes to six and the congregation consisted only of Fred and Marcie. He turned to Betty May and announced, "Listen, I'm sorry, but I think I better get started back to Charleston. The way this ice is coming down, there's no telling how long it's going to take to . . . ."

"No!" objected Gertie. "You can't leave. It's Christmas Eve. You've got to lead the service. It's *Christmas Eve!*"

Gertie was embarrassed as soon as the words left her mouth. What was she thinking? She didn't want Pastor Schultz to end up in a ditch or over some hillside. But before she could apologize for her outburst, Pastor Schultz was off to answer the phone.

Pastor Schultz soon returned with a greater look of concern than before mixed with a tinge of disappointment. "That was the Clerk of Session from First Church. She said to stay put. The ice is really piling up. They've closed the main highway from here to Charleston. The highway patrol has declared a state of emergency. There are accidents all over the place. I guess nobody's going to have a service tonight. Could things get any worse?"

The words had barely left the pastor's lips when things did get worse. Much worse. The lights went out! The candles in the windows provided a faint light that allowed the occupants of the sanctuary to find their way around. While Pastor Schultz fumbled down the hallway to phone his wife and assure her that he was okay, Gertie went to the window and peered outside. She noticed that everything was dark.

"Power's out everywhere," she shouted to whomever was listening.

"Yes ma'am," agreed Jeb, "and as bad as this storm is getting, I reckon it's going to be some time before they get the power back on. Sure glad we have this wood burner."

"Why Jeb?" asked Gertie. "What difference does it make? Our furnace isn't electric. It burns oil."

"Sure enough, Miss Gertie," acknowledged Jeb, "but the furnace won't run without electricity because the blower is electric."

Gertie shook her head, recognizing that what Jeb said made sense even if she had never thought about it before. Then, all of a sudden, her head stopped shaking and her eyes got big. She looked out the window toward the new housing development only to see sheer darkness. There were no gawdy lights on the outside, and, thought Gertie, no heat on the inside.

"Jeb, why don't you and Fred go over to those new houses and invite folks to come on over to the church. You've got it toasty warm over here and I'm afraid there are an awful lot of youngsters over there facing a mighty chill. There are a couple of flashlights in the back room."

Without a word, Jeb motioned to Fred and the two of them headed for the back room. Two beams of light signaled that the flashlights had been found, and the two rescuers slipped on their coats and carefully made their way out of the door.

Pastor Schultz followed them. Standing at the door, he shouted for them to have people bring some blankets and pillows. "It could be a long night," he warned.

Within ten minutes, the first of the unexpected guests arrived. Before long nine young moms with children in tow arrived, leaving husbands to hold down the fort. An air of confusion was mixed with words of appreciation for the emergency hospitality.

Once the children warmed up and dried off a little, the whining began. What was going to happen to Christmas? Could Santa Claus fly in an ice storm? Why weren't the pretty lights on anymore? Some were hungry while others were bored.

Gertie had an idea.

"Pastor, look around," she said. Pastor Schultz looked out into the sanctuary lit with flickering candles and realized that, counting Fred and Marcie, there were eleven adults and sixteen children filling the pews of the sanctuary. Gertie looked at her watch. It was now 7:11 p.m. "Pastor," said Gertie, "I think it's past time for the candlelight service."

Pastor Schultz walked over to Betty May and whispered something in her ear. Betty May picked up her music and sat down at the piano. Quietly, she began to play her prelude. Pastor Schultz walked to the pulpit and asked for everyone's attention.

"Folks, welcome! We were just about to begin our candlelight service when this storm hit and the power went out. We have enough candles to light up the sanctuary and I wonder if you would like to join us."

Having no alternative forms of entertainment available, a young teenage boy in the corner spoke for the group. "Sure, why not? What else we got to do?"

Pastor Schultz was hoping for a more enthusiastic response, but he settled for the half-hearted assent. Opening his worship folder, Pastor Schultz began the service. Scripture readings were followed by Christmas carols and then prayers. Finally, Pastor Schultz got to the evening message. He came to the steps, sat down, and asked if the children would like to join him. Most of the children did. Pastor Schultz pulled out a picture book describing the first Christmas. He opened the book and began to tell the Christmas story. They were all there—the angels, the shepherds, the sheep, Mary and Joseph, and, of course, the baby Jesus. About halfway through the story, Pastor Schultz became aware that the congregation was captivated. Parents listened as attentively as the children. The children strained their necks to look at the picture on each page. When Pastor Schultz finished the story, one of the children commented, "That was a really good story."

"That was a *true* story," responded Pastor Schultz. "It's the story about how God's Son became human like you and me. He came because people weren't always doing what was right and it made God very sad. God wanted to change their hearts because God loved them so much. God loves us so much. And so, God sent Jesus."

"I've heard of him," one of the children blurted out, "but I'm not sure where."

"We learn about Jesus in the Bible," responded Pastor Schultz, "and if you come back some time, I'll tell you more about him and the wonderful things he does for us."

When the message ended and the children returned to their seats, Betty May slowly and quietly played the introduction to "Silent Night, Holy Night." Candles were distributed and the sanctuary came alive with light. The children looked around with wonder and the little impromptu congregation began to sing the familiar words. When the hymn ended, the pastor said a benediction, candles were extinguished, and a gentle silence fell on the group.

But not for long. Within minutes little voices were again whining. "I'm hungry," and "I'm bored," were repeated all over the sanctuary. Frustrated moms tried to convince their little ones that it might be a good idea to use a pew as a bed, but the children were clearly in no mood for sleep. That's when Gertie got an idea.

"Jeb, come with me," requested Gertie, and she headed for the narthex to put on her coat.

Jeb followed behind, protesting that it was too dangerous to try to walk on the ice. Slowly and carefully, Gertie and Jeb eased their way across the road and into Gertie's house. With Jeb holding the flashlight, Gertie went through the cupboards, gathering items and placing them in a box. Giving the box to Jeb, Gertie took the flashlight and led the way back across the street and into the church.

When Gertie opened the door of the sanctuary, she discovered that whining had given way to crying children and cross mothers. Gertie motioned for Jeb to head for the basement while she walked to the front of the sanctuary.

"Children, I understand that you are hungry and bored. I think I can do something about both of these problems. Follow me," she declared.

Parents and children alike started down the stairway lit by the beams of several flashlights. Pastor Schultz followed with Fred and Marcie close behind, curious as to what Gertie was up to.

The basement was already lit by several candles and an old kerosene lamp. From one corner came a strange flickering light and the smell of burning wood. One young woman walked over in that direction and exclaimed, "What do you know, a wood-burning stove with an oven! I didn't know these things existed anymore."

Gertie didn't let on that the stove was only occasionally used to warm the basement and that she had never tried to bake in it. She directed the bored and hungry gathering to several nearby tables she carefully covered with plastic tablecloths. Mixing bowls, measuring cups, spoons, and a variety of ingredients were placed on each table. The last thing to come out of the box brought from home was a cookbook. She quickly turned to a familiar page and began giving directions. Water was hand-pumped into measuring cups from a nearby sink. Hands were floured. Balls of dough were rolled out. Cookie cutters cut out people shapes that were quickly transferred to cookie sheets. Candies and raisins created faces and buttons. Then into the oven they went. Before they knew it, gingerbread people covered the table. Some were a little burned around the edges and others were slightly doughy in the middle. Some were missing an arm or a leg. Still others had misshapen heads. But to the children and adults gathered in the old church basement that night, it didn't matter. They were beautiful creations of love.

"Who's hungry?" Gertie asked with a grin.

The children's hands shot up along with Jeb's and Fred's. Gertie revealed a gallon of milk she had brought from home. Glasses and cups were pulled from the cupboard, rinsed out, and filled with the cool white liquid. Smacking lips were a common sound for the next few minutes.

While Jeb, Fred, and Marcie helped Gertie clean up, Pastor Schultz and Betty May led the refreshed group back up the stairs to the sanctuary. Pews were converted to beds and children were soon falling off to sleep with visions of gingerbread people dancing in their heads and stomachs.

One tired young woman approached Gertie. "Thank you so much," she said putting her arm around Gertie. "That was so much fun. I haven't done that since I was a little girl. My husband and I work all week, but I have some free time during the weekends. Do you think you could teach me how to bake?"

"Only if you bring the children along," Gertie responded with a smile.

"And Pastor," she continued. Gertie turned around to discover Pastor Schultz listening in on her conversation. "I want my children to hear more about Jesus. It's been a long time since I've been to church, but I'm going to be back and so are the kids. I'll work on my husband too."

By eleven o'clock, both adults and children were drifting off to sleep. As Gertie nodded off on a pew, she thought that this must be what the Christmas carol meant by "Sleep in heavenly peace."

Suddenly the lights turned on and the group awakened with a start. Gertie rubbed her eyes and looked at the wind-up clock on the wall. It was 5:25 a.m. Christmas morning! Soon adults and children all over the sanctuary were stirring. Blankets and pillows were gathered. Young men showed up at the church door to retrieve their families. One by one, they made their way out the door and headed for their homes. As the last family went to leave, a little girl walked up to Gertie and pulled on her blouse.

"Hey lady," she said. "Here, this is for you. Merry Christmas."

Gertie took something wrapped in a napkin from the child's little hand. She opened it, and there was a gingerbread person. One arm was missing and the smile created by raisins was crooked; but to Gertie it was the most precious Christmas gift she had received that Christmas. Gertie bent down and gave the child a kiss on the cheek.

"Merry Christmas, and thank you," Gertie uttered, her eyes a little blurred and wet.

"Hey lady, can I come back here sometime and can we make gingerbread people again?"

Gertie nodded. "You bet. You can come here any time you want to make gingerbread people and to hear more stories about Jesus."

"Good," she responded through sleepy eyes. "Now I have to go home and see if Santa Claus came to my house."

And off went the young family toward their home, again ablaze with twinkle lights.

Gertie looked down at the cookie in her hand. She looked up at her pastor, saw his disheveled hair and that he was in need of a shave.

"Pastor," she said, "I think maybe you better plan on spending more time around here. It looks like your Narrow Ridge congregation might be coming back to life. And if you need someone to work with the children, you know where to find me."

With that, Gertie started slowly across the road toward her house, a cookie in one hand and a song of Christmas joy in her heart.

Questions for Reflection and Discussion

1. Why do you think fewer young families are attending church?

2. How do Gertie's actions reveal the love of Christ?

3. What might you or your church do to connect with people in your neighborhood with the spirit of Christ's love?

13. A Part for Freddy

R uth Thompson had a problem. It all began the Sunday after Thanksgiving, the night of the Christmas play tryouts. Ruth had advertised in the church newsletter and bulletin that all the children of the church were invited to tryout for various parts in the Christmas play. Ruth had a reputation for being a perfectionist; but, after all, she did present the best Christmas play in town year after year. For fourteen years she had directed the Christmas play in her church and she took special pride in this annual production. She spent weeks on the sets, hand-painting every detail. She carefully prepared the scripts, proofreading each page so that there were no errors. One of the women's circles was recruited to prepare the costumes according to her rigid specifications. Everything had to be right. Everything had to be perfect. Then and only then could she settle into her routine of finding the right children to fill each part and prepare them to become characters in the Christmas story.

As usual, the turnout was good and there were plenty of children to fill the parts. The children were ushered into the large fellowship hall with a stage at one end. Parents were strictly forbidden from watching and everyone knew that Mrs. Thompson's decisions were final and irreversible.

Ruth observed the group of children who had gathered. They looked like good prospects. She could already see her main characters. There was Elizabeth—she had been a magnificent Mary the past two years. There was Mark, the perfect Joseph. His mother had informed Ruth that Mark had been practicing for the past two months. Ruth loved the fact that the children took the play so seriously. It was going to be another great year.

It was then that she noticed one of the children who stood out and stood apart. He was a little boy, about eight years old she guessed, with Down Syndrome. He stared at the floor with a bit of a pout on his face. A girl about the same age as the boy walked over to him, took him by the hand, and led him over to where Ruth was standing.

"Mrs. Thompson," she said, "this is Freddy."

"Frederick Charles Taylor the Third," he chimed in, "but you can call me Freddy."

Ruth immediately noticed his rather serious speech impediment, though she was able to make out what he was trying to say. "Thank you, Susan, for introducing Freddy to me," Ruth responded. "I don't think I've met Freddy before."

Susan replied, "That's because he's new in town. He and his mother live across the street from me. They said they're going to start going to church here."

"I want to be in the play," interrupted Freddy.

Ruth swallowed hard, thought for a moment and answered, "Of course. Most children who come to tryouts for the first time sing in the Cherub Choir. Mrs. McCormick, right over there, is having tryouts."

Ruth pointed to a young woman standing in one corner of the room talking to several children. Susan took Freddy by the hand and started walking in Mrs. McCormick's direction.

Now Ruth set out to complete her task. She announced a part and asked which children would like to tryout. No one seemed ready to challenge Elizabeth for the part of Mary or Mark for the role of Joseph. Wise men and shepherds seemed to be popular roles and several readings took place before Ruth could determine which children would receive the parts. Scripts were handed out and instructions for practicing at home were given. Just as Ruth was choosing the last shepherd, Mrs. McCormick interrupted.

"Ruth, can I speak with you for just a moment . . . privately?"

"Sure, Sarah," she replied. Something appeared to be wrong and Ruth was anxious to find out what it could be.

"It's about Freddy," she whispered. "He can't carry a tune in a bucket. He's way off-key and sings much louder than the other children. When he doesn't know the words, and that's most of the time, he makes them up. The other children were starting to laugh at him and, well, it's just not working."

"Bring him over here," Ruth responded, somewhat annoyed and with a touch of frustration in her voice. Freddy was brought to her and she forced her best smile.

"Freddy, I still have a part available. It's an important part. Would you like to tryout for it?"

Freddy's face lit up and he nodded so hard his glasses slipped from his face. Ruth took out the script and handed it to Freddy. The lines were highlighted in yellow. It was the simplest speaking part in the play. All he had to say was, "There is no room in my inn, but you may use the stable in the back."

Freddy looked confused. He was staring at the floor again.

"Mrs. Thompson," a voice interrupted. It was Susan again. "He can't read very good, Mrs. Thompson. He goes to the special class at school. He's a really nice boy and he's my friend, but he can't read much."

Ruth tried even harder to force a smile. What was she to do? Why was this child here? How was she going to find a part for Freddy?

It was then that Ruth had an idea, a brainstorm. She reached down and took the boy by the hand. "Freddy," she said with a big smile, "do I have a job for you."

"A job?" repeated Freddy. "For me?"

"That's right," Ruth answered. "You are going to be our stage manager."

Freddy looked even more confused than before. He didn't have to say a word. It was clear Freddy didn't have the foggiest idea what a stage manager was.

Ruth tried to assure Freddy. "You'll really like being a stage manager. You'll be my right-hand man. You'll help get the stage ready for the play, hand out the scripts, help with the costumes. It's a very important job."

Ruth wasn't sure who she was trying harder to convince, Freddy or herself.

Freddy raised his eyes from the floor and inquired, "Really? It's important?"

"It is," answered Ruth, "it really is."

"Come on, Freddy. It's time to go home."

It was Susan again. She grabbed Freddy's hand and the two headed for the door. Ruth looked over at Sarah McCormick and winked.

"I think we pulled it off," she said in a low voice.

Sarah smiled back with approval.

Rehearsal began in earnest, scheduled three times a week—Wednesday evenings, Saturday mornings, and Sunday evenings. All children were expected to be there on time. As always, the parents cooperated and rehearsals went extraordinarily well. Ruth was convinced this would be the finest play she had directed; and that was saying a lot.

It was the Wednesday evening before the performance. Ruth had just walked in the door and hung up her coat when she noticed she had a voicemail. She listened and heard, "Mrs. Thompson, this is Mrs. Taylor, Freddy's mother. I'm sorry to bother you, but"—there was a moment of silence as though she was trying to compose herself—"would you please call me back when you get this?" She gave her phone number. Ruth wrote it down.

Ruth sat by the phone for the longest time staring at the phone number. What could this be about? There hadn't been any problems with Freddy. Had one of the children called him a name or made fun of him? If so, she hadn't noticed.

Ruth dialed the phone and it began to ring. On the eighth ring Ruth prepared to hang up when she heard a woman's voice answer.

"Hello, Mrs. Taylor?" asked Ruth.

"Yes, that's me," responded the voice.

"This is Ruth Thompson returning your call."

"Oh, Mrs. Thompson." A moment of silence. "Thanks for calling back." More silence. "I'm sorry to bother you but, it's about Freddy. He's really upset."

Ruth could tell that Freddy's mother was struggling to hold back tears. "Mrs. Thompson, are you sure? He's been so cooperative and seems to be having a good time."

"That's not what I'm hearing," answered Freddy's mother. "He had his heart set on getting a part in the Christmas play. It's all he talked about from the day Pastor Janet announced your tryouts in church."

"Mrs. Taylor, I understand your disappointment, but . . ."

"No," interrupted the young woman, "I don't think you do. Freddy is my life. When Freddy was born, his father walked out on us. He left me and Freddy to fend for ourselves. Well, we do pretty good, but sometimes it's hard."

"Mrs. Taylor," responded Ruth, "I didn't mean to offend you or Freddy. It's just that I have a job to do and it's hard to make choices. The choices must be for the good of the play and the good of the church. What would happen if we sacrificed the whole play for one child?"

"But Mrs. Thompson," there was anger in her voice this time, "my Freddy loves Jesus. He really loves Jesus. Every night before he goes to bed, he walks over to our nativity scene, he ever so carefully picks up the baby Jesus, he kisses it goodnight, and he says, 'I love you baby Jesus.'"

Ruth assured the upset mother that she had done everything she could and that she appreciated Freddy's help as stage manager. The young mother politely said, "Thank you anyway," and the conversation ended.

Ruth sat in her kitchen nursing a cup of coffee. She thought about the conversation with Freddy's mother. *How unreasonable,* she thought. Why couldn't she see that Ruth had done what she had to do?

Ruth picked up the phone. She needed to hear a reassuring voice and have someone she respected confirm her decision. The call rang through and a cheerful voice greeted her.

"Janet, it's Ruth."

Janet Williams had been the pastor of the church a little over three years. Originally, Ruth didn't like the idea of a woman pastor, but it wasn't long before Janet changed her perspective. She now bragged that her church had the best pastor in the history of the town.

"Ruth, I think I know why you're calling. I spoke earlier this evening with Fran Taylor. She said she might call you."

Ruth chimed in. "Can you believe the nerve of that woman? Expecting me to change all my plans so close to the performance of the Christmas play? We have dress rehearsal in just three days."

There was a brief moment of silence and then Janet responded. "Ruth, I don't know how to say this, but I think we need to try and do something. This is a special case and may require special allowances. Isn't there some small part without any speaking required? A sheep or a donkey or something that Freddy could play?"

Ruth couldn't believe her ears. She had called her pastor in order to get a little comfort, and instead she was getting more grief.

"Reverend Williams," Ruth stated firmly, "It is too late. All the costumes have been fitted and the parts have been assigned. I've done everything I can."

"Of course you have," Janet responded. Her tone of voice was conciliatory. "I'm sorry to have challenged your decision. I'm sure the play will be outstanding as always." After an exchange of pleasantries, the conversation ended.

Ruth walked into her living room and plopped down on her favorite chair. Confused and frustrated, she picked up her Bible. She turned to the Christmas story in Luke chapter 2. As she read, these words jumped out at her: "And she gave birth to her firstborn son and wrapped him in bands of cloth, and laid him in a manger, because there was no place for them in the inn."[1]

She laid the Bible down.

---

1. Luke 2:7.

No room.

No room for the holy family.

No room for the baby Jesus.

No room for Freddy in her play.

Something was wrong, but she didn't know how to make it right. She thought of her conversation with Freddy's mother. She pictured Freddy in her mind, and she got an idea—a part for Freddy.

The day of the Christmas play arrived. As usual Ruth was nervous, but also confident that all would go well. The sanctuary was filled to capacity as the choir began to sing, "Joy to the World." Joseph and Mary entered the sanctuary and started up the steps to the chancel level. That's when Ruth noticed Elizabeth pulling up her robe. It took a moment before Ruth could figure out what she was doing. She was showing off her new shiny leather shoes and bright green Christmas socks. Joseph was so startled by Mary's exhibition that he tripped over the top step. Frantically reaching out as he fell, he knocked over Mary who bumped into the manger, tipping it over.

Once the holy family composed themselves, the shepherds entered leading their sheep. Each year the kindergarten children were given the part of the sheep and this was "a particularly active group of children," as their Sunday school teacher described them. The sheep were a bit unruly, running back and forth in front of the chancel. One overly zealous shepherd yelled, "Stop it," and poked a rowdy sheep a bit too hard with his staff. A loud "Ow" could be heard followed by a high-pitched squeal and an outburst of tears. The wounded sheep went racing down the center aisle of the sanctuary, wailing and searching for the comfort of a parent.

Now it was time for the wise men to make their appearance and Ruth couldn't believe her eyes. Instead of the three wise men, they turned out to be the three wise guys. Giggling uncontrollably, they entered wearing, not the carefully crafted crowns prepared by the women's circle, but cardboard crowns from the local fast-food restaurant; and instead of gold, frankincense, and myrrh, they presented the baby Jesus with the empty packaging for a burger, fries, and a soft drink. The parents of three boys were clearly not amused with the exception of one father who started laughing. The scowl on his wife's face suggested that not only three boys, but also one husband, were going to receive a scolding.

Ruth slumped down in her seat. For the first time, her Christmas play was a disaster. Everything that could go wrong had gone wrong. She was so preoccupied with her self-pity that she almost forgot the final act. After everything she had been through, she didn't want to forget Freddy's part. She motioned to one of the ushers who obligingly exited by the side door and reappeared, gently shoving Freddy into the sanctuary. Freddy was dressed in his best shirt and pants and was wearing a Christmas bow tie his mother had made for him. In his arms was a large red heart cut out of poster board. He walked slowly toward the manger scene. He knelt at the manger and picked up the baby doll playing the role of the infant Jesus. He gently kissed it and said, "I love you, baby Jesus."

He smiled sheepishly and exited by the same door he had entered. The congregation sat in silence for what seemed like a long time. Then the applause began. Finally, Ruth's humiliating experience was over.

Ruth dodged a few parents who congratulated her, thanked the pastor for her words of encouragement, and left the church as quickly as she could. Ruth had never felt such embarrassment. She had worked so hard and the play had gone so poorly. Her pride and joy had become a public disgrace. She wanted the congregation to be inspired, and at best they were amused by what had happened. She wondered how she would ever show her face in church again.

There are moments in life when we come to realize that a seemingly insignificant decision we have made has had a transformational effect on the lives of others. Ruth experienced such a moment at the Christmas Eve service just two days after the Christmas play fiasco. The service was lovely as always and ended with the singing of "Silent Night" by candlelight. It was the practice of the congregation to pass by the manger on their way out of the sanctuary following the benediction. Ruth got in line and made her way toward the manger. When she arrived at the front of the church, she stopped in amazement. There, surrounding the manger, were what seemed like hundreds of paper hearts of every size and color. And on each heart were written the words, "I love you, baby Jesus."

Freddy had found his part and done his part to remind a congregation and an overly zealous Christmas play director what really matters.

Questions for Reflection and Discussion

1. How can we relate to persons with disabilities in ways that honor their dignity and worth?

2. What accommodations for persons with disabilities do you see in your community and congregation? What more could you do?

3. What is it about Freddy's simple act that so touches the hearts of the congregation?

14. Home for Christmas

The windshield wipers in the rental car clicked in time with a Christmas song on the car radio. The lyrics brought a bit of a smile to Ray's face as he recalled the sounds, sights, and smells of being home for Christmas. It had been a year since he had last stepped inside that familiar house that was home. His job kept him too busy to get away, he would always say. He was the youngest vice president the company had ever had. They expected more of him, he would explain, when his mother would ask that uncomfortable question, "When are you coming home?" But Christmas was the one exception, the one time during the year when there were no excuses.

As Ray drove from the airport to his hometown, he thought about those childhood Christmases in Winthrop, Minnesota with his older sister and younger brother. He and Bill would sneak over to Jean's room to see if she was awake yet. She always was but pretended she wasn't. She'd complain that they woke her up, that it was too early to get their parents out of bed, but before long she wasn't able to contain herself either.

Their giggling worked like an alarm clock every Christmas morning. Mom and Dad would appear in the doorway of Jean's room, red-eyed and in their robes.

"Are you kids up already?" they would ask. "It's only six o'clock."

But soon they had them convinced that if they didn't go downstairs to check if Santa had come, they would burst. So, down the stairs they would bound and, of course, the gifts were always piled high under the tree.

They would all be there tonight when he arrived home—Jean and her family, Bill and his new wife, Dad, Mom, and Grandma. There would be the usual hugs and greetings and a dinner unlike any other, and then they would go to church for the candlelight service. They always had for as long as Ray could remember.

It seemed strange to Ray that he should want to attend a church service so much. He had gone to church with his family as a boy, but as he had grown older he had drifted away from it. He was so busy and Sunday was the one day he had to himself. Anyway, so many of the church people he had known didn't seem to live any better because of it. So why did he want to attend a church service on this night? He couldn't think of a reason except that it was part of being home for Christmas.

A high-pitched sound on the car radio caught his attention. The national weather service was issuing a winter storm warning with blowing and drifting snow and an additional eight to twelve inches of accumulation. Ray noticed that the snow was falling harder and the highway appeared as little more than two sets of tire tracks. Snow didn't frighten someone who had grown up in Minnesota and was now living in Denver, but he had learned when driving was hazardous and that time had come. Ray slowed down.

Suddenly he noticed taillights flashing up ahead of him. As he came nearer, he saw an old pick-up truck that had skidded off the road and into a ditch. A man was standing by the truck, waving his arms frantically. Ray hesitantly stopped the car, aware that any delay would make him late getting home for Christmas.

"Can I call you a tow truck?" Ray offered.

"No time!" the man responded, half out of breath, half-panicky. "My wife, please," he pleaded. Ray looked over at the truck and noticed that a woman was still seated in it. "We were on our way to the hospital when we got stuck in the ditch," he explained.

"Why, is someone ill?" Ray asked.

Just then the woman stepped out of the truck. Even with a coat on, it was obvious this woman was going to have a baby and soon. Ray couldn't help but notice that the woman's coat, like the pick-up, was in disrepair.

"Joe, I think we better hurry," she pleaded.

Ray jumped from the car without hesitation. "Come on," he assured them, "I'll take you to the hospital."

Ray assisted the woman as she entered the back seat while her husband went to the truck, returning with a tattered cloth suitcase. He jumped in the back seat and off they went. Ray accelerated carefully, for the road was barely visible.

"I'm Ray Schmidt," he said, looking into the rearview mirror. Although it was growing dark, he could see that his passengers were frightened.

"I'm Joe Carpenter," a voice uttered nervously from the back seat. "This is my wife, Mary Louise. She's going to have a baby."

"Yes, I kind of guessed that," Ray replied with a chuckle. There were quiet groans and hard breathing from the back.

"How far to the nearest hospital?" Ray inquired.

"About 35 miles straight ahead," Joe responded. They drove in silence for a short time; although the silence seemed to be broken more and more frequently by sounds of discomfort.

"I don't think we're going to make it," a frightened voice suddenly exclaimed.

Ray tried to speed up, but nearly lost control of the car. That's when Ray spotted it just ahead—a little white frame country church with cars parked around it. Instinctively, Ray pulled off the road and stopped at the church. "

I'm going to get help," he assured his passengers, and he hurried to a door where he saw lights. He walked in to find thirty to forty people sitting around candlelit tables eating their dinner. A man about Ray's age walked toward him.

"Hi, I'm the pastor here, Roger Lewis," he said. "Can I help you?"

Ray told the pastor about what had happened as quickly as he could. The pastor motioned toward a woman sitting at a table in the corner.

"Hey Doc, would you come here please?"

The woman rose and approached them. The pastor whispered something to her and things began to happen. The doctor directed two men to help the Carpenters into the church. The pastor cleared space in his study. The room filled with families began to buzz. Before long Joe and Mary Louise were in the study and the doctor was poking her head out saying, "Tell Jim I'll need my things."

The pastor spoke to a tall man who left and quickly returned with the doctor's case. Others were also leaving and soon arrived back with a basinet, baby clothes, and diapers.

"Would you like something to eat?" asked an older woman. "There's plenty."

"Everything looks very good," Ray responded, "but I have to get going if I'm going to make it home for Christmas Eve."

"I'm afraid you're not going anywhere tonight," interrupted a man who had overheard. "A tractor trailer jack-knifed up the road a couple of miles. They've closed the highway. Anyway, it's a blizzard out there. Why don't you call your family and tell them you're okay?"

Ray made his phone call. He explained his situation and that he was safe. His family understood and hoped he could travel safely in the morning.

Ray ate some leftovers from the church dinner. People were beginning to leave and several families offered him a place to stay the night. Each time he declined, saying that he wanted to make sure everything turned out alright for his passengers.

The doctor stepped out of the study and motioned to the pastor.

"We've got some complications," she said. "Call my nurse, Cindy, and tell her I need her pronto."

In a matter of minutes, a woman hurried into the church hall and disappeared into the study. Ray watched what was happening with concern on his face.

Roger Lewis sat down beside him. "I'm sorry you're not going to make it home for Christmas tonight. That snow is really coming down. I've sent our folks home. First time in a long time we haven't been able to hold our candlelight service."

"Do you think they'll be okay?" Ray asked.

"Doctor Shannon is a fine doctor. She knows her stuff," he assured Ray. "But I'm sure she can use our prayers," he added.

Ray kept his vigil that night. As he sat there alone, he wondered why he had stopped at that church that night. And then, he knew why. There, that night, Ray Schmidt did what he hadn't done for a long time. He prayed. He prayed for a mother and child who were strangers but seemed to matter to him almost like family.

As the night wore on, he hummed some Christmas carols while munching on leftover cookies. He walked over to a box containing candles and took one. Reaching into his pocket, he pulled out his lighter and lit the candle. Then, quietly, he began to sing, "Silent night, holy night; all is calm, all is bright. Round yon virgin, mother and child; holy infant so tender and mild. Sleep in heavenly peace, sleep in heavenly peace."

At seven minutes after midnight a baby's cry broke the silence. In the early hours of Christmas morning a baby was born— a girl. They named her Angel Noel because, as her parent put it, she was their Christmas angel.

But something else happened that Christmas morning—a child of God realized once again that he was a child of God.

Snowbound in a country church, Ray Schmidt knew he had come home for Christmas.

Questions for Reflection and Discussion

1. Imagine you are in a conversation with Ray. He comments that so many of the church people he had known didn't seem to live any better because of it. How would you respond?

2. Ray stops almost instinctively at a church for help? Why?

3. What gives new life to Ray's dormant faith?

15. The Christmas Snow

It was the first Christmas Naomi had looked forward to since Jake's death nearly three years earlier. She had climbed into the attic and brought down all of the decorations, trimmed a freshly cut tree, strung pine roping with carefully spaced red bows along the banister on the front porch, hung a great wreath on the door, and placed an inviting electric candle in each window. She even hung mistletoe in the entryway.

Naomi's Christmas spirit was due to the much-anticipated arrival of her family for four glorious days. Her daughter Jean, son-in-law Charles, and grandchildren Madison (age 10), Aaron (age 7), and little Lucy (age 3), would leave the next day to travel from Chicago to the farmlands of Flat Rock, Ohio. The trip took less than a day by car, but busy schedules made family homecomings rather rare. Naomi thought how good it would be to have someone to fuss over.

Naomi still missed Jake, but sometimes she thought she missed being needed even more. The big old farmhouse gave her plenty to do, what with cleaning, dusting, and making minor repairs, but caring for an empty house seemed a thankless job. There were neighbors nearby, but even country folks didn't visit like they used to. Loneliness was a frequent companion for Naomi, but for the next four days Naomi could chase her old nemesis away. As Naomi prepared for bed that night, she carefully checked that all way ready. Cookies had been baked, the turkey was nearly thawed, and the gifts were wrapped and under the tree. Yes, she had everything prepared and on schedule. Still, like an excited child on the night before Christmas, Naomi found it hard to drift off to sleep.

Naomi rose early on December 24. She thought to herself as she dressed that her family would be leaving for Flat Rock in a few hours. Naomi lifted the shade and, although the sun had not yet risen, she could faintly make out tiny flakes drifting from the sky. She went to the front door, turned on the light, and beheld a wisp of white dustlike snow across the porch. A look of concern replaced her girlish smile. *No time to stand here and fret*, she thought to herself. There were beds to be made up and pies to bake. Her family would be there before nightfall and she must be ready for them.

By nine o'clock the beds were made, fresh towels were hung in the bathrooms, and the smell of baking pies filled the house. Naomi sat down with a second cup of coffee and looked apprehensively out the window. The dustlike snow had now become great flakes which were falling harder. Naomi noticed she could no longer see the ground, and the church across the field was rendered nearly invisible behind a sheet of white.

Naomi was startled by the timer on the stove announcing that pies were ready to be cooled. She had just placed the pies on the table when the phone rang—once, twice, three times. Naomi stood frozen, like a cornered rabbit hoping that a predator might just go away. By the sixth ring she reached the phone and hesitantly said, "Hello."

"Mom. It's Jean. Would you believe we're snowed in up here? We have eight inches of snow on the ground and another six predicted. They've even closed a section of the turnpike. Mom, I'm sorry."

"Honey, don't give it a second thought," she heard herself saying. "All that matters is your safety."

"Mom, Charlie thinks he can get a long weekend off in February and we'll be down. In the meantime, we'll send your gifts in the mail." After a moment she said, "We're really disappointed."

"Me too," responded Naomi, "but it's all right. Now you have a Merry Christmas and give those children a big kiss for me."

Goodbyes were exchanged and the line at the other end went dead. Naomi replaced the receiver. She stood there in a fog. Like someone just awakened from a nightmare, she wondered if it all could be true. She looked around, noticing how pleasant the house appeared. If only it felt that way. The silence was deafening. A single tear made its way down her cheek.

The rest of the day was filled with busyness. By nightfall she had straightened up all the kitchen cupboards, reorganized the books on her bookshelf, and rearranged her closet. Perhaps if she kept busy, she could avoid the ache deep inside.

That evening Naomi sat at the table and picked at her dinner. She stared out the window at the still-falling snow. Each flake seemed like a little demon ruining her Christmas and mocking her pain.

It was then her eyes fell on the Bible sitting on the coffee table. She picked it up and ran her fingers over the cover. Noticing an old Christmas bookmark, she opened to the page in which it had been placed. Naomi began to read, "For God so loved the world that he gave his only Son, so that everyone who believes in him may not perish but may have eternal life. Indeed, God did not send the Son into the word to condemn the world, but in order that the world might be saved through him."[1]

Naomi thought about how God's love had carried her through those agonizing months after Jake's death. She remembered times when she felt like she was drowning in grief, sure she could not go on. On the edge of despair, she sensed that God's hand was reaching down to save her. While her family's absence brought back some of those feelings, draining the joy out of her Christmas plans, she still sensed that, somehow, God would provide a Christmas blessing.

Little did she know how right she was.

Naomi looked out the window. A single set of headlights cutting through the darkness caught Naomi's attention. As the car

1. John 3:16–17.

came to the bend in the road, it suddenly stopped. Naomi knew immediately what had happened. A ditch along the road, rendered invisible by drifting snow, had swallowed another car. Naomi watched as a group of figures emerged from the car and slowly made their way up her driveway. Naomi pulled on her coat and walked out onto the porch to meet her unexpected guests. As they stepped into the glimmer of the porch light, she could make out a young African American man and woman with three children, one in her father's arms.

"Ma'am, I'm sorry to bother you, but I seem to be stuck in a ditch. May I use your phone?"

Naomi hesitated for a moment, then responded, "Come inside. The phone is over there. Now let's get your children out of these snowy things and warm them up."

The young woman removed her coat, hung it over a chair and began to undress the youngest. "I'm Alisha Barrett," she said. "We're sure sorry to break in on your Christmas Eve."

"I'm Naomi Brown and don't give it a second thought," she responded with a warm smile. "That ditch has led more motorists to my door over the years than I can remember. What brings you out on a night like this?"

"My husband Daniel has been out of work for six months. An old friend in Pittsburgh promised him a job and a place to stay if he could start the day after Christmas."

"The tow truck's coming," interrupted Daniel. "I'm going out to meet him. Thanks for your hospitality, ma'am. We'll be on our way soon," he said as he looked reassuringly at his wife. He pulled up his collar and stepped outside.

Naomi commented, "Your children are beautiful. What are their names?"

Pointing to each child, Alisha responded proudly, "This is Talisha, Tyrell, and our youngest, Tamyra. We call them Tali, Ty, and Tami for short."

Naomi, smiling, said, "They remind me of my grandchildren. Two girls and a boy and about the same ages." There was a faraway look in her eyes.

Yellow lights flashing along the road indicated the arrival of the tow truck. Alisha stood at the window and watched as the car was pulled from the ditch. A few moments later the truck pulled out with the car in tow. Her husband walked up the driveway with a look of dejection on his face and suitcases in hand. He shook off the snow and stepped inside. "The tie rod is bent. He thinks he can fix it and have it ready some time tomorrow," Daniel mumbled.

"Then you'll stay here tonight," Naomi responded. "Have you had your dinner?"

Suddenly the house was filled with activity. The children huddled around the television. Daniel and Alisha helped Naomi prepare a meal for the young family. Once everyone was fed, suitcases were taken upstairs and travel-weary children were put to bed. Soon the young parents returned downstairs and joined Naomi in the living room by the Christmas tree.

"We are sorry to interrupt your Christmas Eve plans," apologized Daniel. "I hope it's not too much of an imposition."

Naomi told the couple how the Christmas snow had spoiled her plans. "The house seemed so empty before your arrival," Naomi said. "If your trip had to be delayed, I'm glad you ended up here. But I am sorry your children's Christmas has been ruined."

Alisha looked at Daniel. "There wasn't going to be any Christmas this year," he said. "This job means everything for us as a family. Maybe next year we can make it up to them."

The hour grew late and the young parents went upstairs to join their children in sleep. Naomi said goodnight and went to the window. The snow had slowed down to flurries. A single flake fell on the windowpane. Naomi observed its intricate beauty and perfect symmetry. She thought of how God so often surprised her with beauty in the midst of pain. She reflected on the day's events and marveled at them. Her disappointment had resulted in an opportunity to be needed.

The next morning the young family awoke to a myriad of delicious smells. They came downstairs to find Naomi working furiously in the kitchen. "Merry Christmas," she exclaimed upon spying her guests. "The turkey is in the oven and the breakfast rolls are almost ready. The mechanic called and said we can pick up the car at two o'clock. That should give you plenty of time to get to Pittsburgh before nightfall."

Daniel looked at Alisha sheepishly. "I don't know how we're going to pay for this repair."

Naomi chimed in, "Oh, I explained your situation to Harry, and he said no charge for the tow or repair. I was to tell you Merry Christmas from him."

Daniel's furrowed brow indicated that something was wrong. "That's real kind, but I always pay my way."

"I'm sure you do," Naomi interrupted, "and you'll have plenty of opportunities in the future. But today is Christmas. Speaking of Christmas, bring the children and come into the living room."

Under the tree were the same packages they had seen the night before, but the tags now contained the names of the Barrett family. Naomi looked at Alisha. "Would you hand out the gifts?"

"I don't understand," replied the young woman. "These gifts are for your family."

"And there's plenty of time to replace them and send them off in the mail," announced Naomi. "Now give your children their Christmas presents."

Now the house was alive with the sound of tearing paper and children's squeals. Once the gifts were all opened Naomi ushered them around the table for a Christmas breakfast. She joined hands with her guests, bowed her head, and led them in a prayer: "I thank you God for the Christ child, for Daniel, Alisha, Talisha, Tyrell, and Tamyra, and for the Christmas snow."

Questions for Reflection and Discussion

1. Why do you think Naomi hesitated in her response to the Barrett family as she met them at the door? What do you think she was thinking and feeling?

2. What do you think Naomi learned from her encounter with the Barrett family? What did the Barrett family learn?

3. What opportunities to extend hospitality to people who are not just like you exist in your community and through your church? How might you participate?

16. No Time for Christmas

He sat in front of his computer, staring intently at the screen. His fingers flew over the keyboard. A slight smile came to his face. He was pleased with his work. This was no ordinary sales presentation. His future depended on it, he kept telling himself. For twelve long years he had worked for the company and now his greatest aspiration might just come true—an office upstairs. Paul had dreamed of being a corporate executive ever since college. Now, if he could win this client, the company would surely make him a vice president. Still, he knew he wasn't the only one after the position. In fact, he was the youngest candidate; but that had never stopped him before. If there was something he wanted, he went after it without reservation.

Paul's work was interrupted by a phone call. Without taking his eyes off the screen, he answered.

"Paul, where are you?" asked an angry, frustrated voice on the other end of the line.

Paul glanced at the clock. It was seven forty-five in the evening. "Pam, I'm sorry, but I just wanted to finish this sales presentation before I came home."

"Paul, it's Christmas Eve. Surely tonight you can give some time to your family. You haven't spent fifteen minutes this week with Paul Jr. He misses you and so do I."

"Pam, honey, you know how important this sales presentation is. If I can have it on Mr. Cooper's desk first thing on Thursday morning, I know the vice presidency is mine."

"Is that all that matters to you? We barely see you as it is. What's going to happen if you do get this promotion? Paul, come home please."

"Pam, I'll be there soon. Just let me finish this up."

His statement was met by a long silence.

"In that case, I don't care when you come home."

The line went dead.

Paul slowly hung up the receiver. He stared at the screen in front of him. Why couldn't she understand he was doing it all for them. If he could get this vice presidency, he could buy them anything they wanted. Paul Jr. could go to the college of his choice. For them. It was all for them, and Pam couldn't see it.

Paul picked up his mug and gulped down a mouth full of cold coffee. He had been working hard, maybe too hard. It was then that he noticed the rest of the office was dark. Everyone else, even Mr. Cooper, had gone home. He looked back at the screen and began typing again, but somehow his heart wasn't in it now. The work was going slower. The ideas weren't flowing. His eyes were getting heavy.

Paul slouched in his chair, resting his head on the back. He thought about his family. He remembered how excited he and Pam were at the birth of their son. Could that have been over five years ago? Where had the time gone? His baby was growing up and he had missed most of it. His time with Paul Jr. had usually been in periods of minutes, not hours. And he had been neglecting Pam too. Late-night meetings and business trips take their toll on a marriage, but Pam seemed to understand. Still, lately she had been complaining that she felt like a single parent most of the time.

"But I'm doing it all for them," he pleaded to no one.

Christmas Eve. Oh, how he loved Christmas Eve as a boy. He and his family would go to church. It was the only time of year when he really liked to sing the hymns. He remembered how he would listen intently to the reading of the Christmas story from the Bible and try to imagine what it would have been like to be there with Mary, Joseph, the shepherds, the angels, and the baby Jesus. Finally, his favorite part of the service would come when he would take his candle, watch the flame jump from his father's candle to his own, and everyone would sing "Silent night, holy night." Then it was home for Christmas Eve snacks with the family before bouncing off to bed. A computer was a poor substitute for a family on Christmas Eve.

Paul's thoughts were interrupted by the sound of a baby crying. He lifted his head and noticed a faint light in the outer office. Who could that be? he wondered. Surely the cleaning lady wasn't working on Christmas Eve. He rose slowly to his feet and walked toward the door of his office. He opened the door slowly and cautiously peeked into the outer office. His eyes grew big. The surroundings were unfamiliar. The room was lit with oil lamps. He took a step forward and noticed a couple huddled in one corner. As he came closer, he noticed that the woman was holding a tiny baby, apparently a newborn.

The man stood up and approached Paul, greeting him with the words, "Peace be with you." Then he inquired, "Are you a shepherd?"

"Me, a shepherd?" answered Paul in disbelief. "No, no, I'm Paul. Paul Smithfield," he stammered back.

"I am Joseph from Nazareth, and this is my wife Mary. We are here in Bethlehem for the registration; and just this very night our son was born right here. The woman looked up and smiled warmly at Paul.

"Your son?" responded Paul. "This is the baby Jesus?"

"How did you know his name?" asked Mary. "Did the shepherds tell you?"

"No," answered Paul thoughtfully, "many people have told me his name over the years; but I guess I wasn't listening, or maybe I just forgot."

"You seem troubled, my brother. Is everything all right?" inquired Joseph.

"No," answered Paul, "nothing is right. You see, I too have a son and he is as special to me as your newborn son is to you. But I never have time to be with him. I'm always working, always trying to . . . to . . ."

Paul stopped.

"To what?" asked Joseph. "What is so important that you do not have time to spend with your family?"

"Do you know I've never told my son about you? I've never taken the time to tell Paul Jr. about this holy night and the wonder of your child. I wanted everything and I've forgotten the most important thing," lamented Paul.

Paul walked closer and gazed at the child in his mother's arms. He remembered the words of a hymn, "The hopes and fears of all the years are met in thee tonight."

Then Paul noticed a wristwatch on Mary's arm. A wristwatch? He looked at the time—two-fifteen. Two-fifteen! Paul awoke with a start. His eyes glanced sleepily at the clock on his desk. Two-fifteen a.m. He hurriedly saved what was finished of his sales presentation and switched off the computer. He grabbed his coat and pulled his scarf around his neck. He walked through the dark outer office and pushed the button for the elevator. As he rode down to the main lobby, he thought of his curious dream. It all seemed so real, as real as when he was a little boy sitting in church listening to the minister read the Christmas story from the Bible. The elevator opened and he moved toward the door. The night guard unlocked the door.

"Good night sir, and Merry Christmas," he said.

Paul stopped for a moment and gave a half smile. "Yes, and Merry Christmas to you also."

His face was met by a cold December night. He hurried to his car and drove through empty streets. A light in this house and that indicated a late-night party might still be going on.

It was nearly three a.m. when Paul walked through the door. He crept quietly into the living room. There on the coffee table was a plate of cookies and a glass of milk for Santa along with Paul Jr.'s wish list. He picked it up and read it. It was printed in his best kindergarten handwriting with plenty of coaching from Pam.

Dear Santa, I want Transformers, a remote control car, a tool chest, and my Daddy.

Paul looked intently at the list. Tears welled up in his eyes and a single tear fell on the list in his hand. Paul wiped his eyes, put down the list, and walked upstairs. He looked into Paul Jr.'s room. He was fast asleep. He tiptoed into his own room. Pam was asleep too. He took his pillow and quietly made his way back down the stairs.

Paul Jr. bounded into his mother's room at the first light of day. "Merry Christmas, Mommy," he cried with delight.

Pam opened her eyes and smiled at her son, who could not contain his excitement. "Where's Daddy?"

Pam looked beside her. Paul's pillow was gone. Maybe she had been too hard on Paul on the phone. Either he feared he was in the doghouse or he was so angry with her that he had decided to spend the night on the couch.

"Do you think there is anything under the tree for you?" Pam asked her son.

"Let's go see," he answered; and, taking his mother by the hand, he pulled her toward the stairs.

As they reached the bottom of the stairs and started toward the tree, Pam beheld a scene that brought a smile to her face. There lying under the Christmas tree among the neatly wrapped packages was Paul, a large bow stuck on his head. He was sound asleep.

"Look Paul," Pam said, "I guess Santa read your letter."

Paul opened his eyes and smiled. "Merry Christmas," he mumbled, half-asleep. Paul Jr. bounded over to him and pulled the bow off his head. He gave his father a big kiss and then started tearing into the presents.

"What does all of this mean?" asked Pam with a smile.

"It means some things are going to have to change in my life," Paul answered. "I had forgotten for a while what matters most to me until I was reminded by an old friend."

"Paul, I'm sorry I was so harsh with you on the phone last night, but . . ."

"Pam, don't apologize," interrupted Paul. "I'm the one who is sorry and I don't plan to ever let my family spend Christmas Eve alone again."

Turning to his son, who was removing another Transformer from a box, Paul said, "Son, right after breakfast I want to read to you a story about a baby boy who changed the world and changed my life."

Questions for Reflection and Discussion

1. How do your priorities affect the way you spend your time?

2. What do you think is going on in Paul's mind when he says, "But I'm doing it all for them?" What do you think he is feeling?

3. What would it look like for you to give yourself as a gift to those you consider your family?

Bibliography

Bailey, Kenneth E. *Jesus through Middle Eastern Eyes: Cultural Studies in the Gospels.* Downers Grove, IL: InterVarsity, 2008.

———. *Open Hearts in Bethlehem: A Christmas Drama.* Downers Grove, IL: InterVarsity, 2013.

www.ingramcontent.com/pod-product-compliance
Lightning Source LLC
Chambersburg PA
CBHW060807250626
47162CB00005B/1702